KU-295-943

V: THE PURSUIT OF DIANA

'You're going to stand trial for what your people did to this planet,' Julie said.

'Hah!' Diana barked. 'How fair a trial do you suppose that will be?'

'Probably not fair at all, but that doesn't really matter. You represent the evil that was done to us, and your trial will symbolise our victory over that evil. But more than that, you owe us compensation.'

'You don't think I'm going to co-operate with you, do you?' Diana sneered,

'If we can figure out how to work the conversion machine,' Julie said coldly, 'you may not have a choice.'

The defiance faded slowly from Diana's face.

*The 'V series, published
by New English Library:*

'V' by A. C. Crispin
V: EAST COAST CRISIS by Howard Weinstein & A. C. Crispin
V: THE PURSUIT OF DIANA by Allen Wold

THE PURSUIT OF
DIANA

Allen Wold

NEW ENGLISH LIBRARY

This novel is a work of fiction. Names, characters, places, and incidents are either the product of the author's imagination or are used fictitiously. Any resemblance to actual events or places or persons, living or dead, is entirely coincidental.

First published in the USA in 1984 by Pinnacle Books, Inc.

Copyright © 1984 by Warner Bros., Inc.

All rights reserved. No part of this publication may be reproduced or transmitted, in any form or by any means, without permission of the publishers.

First NEL Paperback Edition June 1985

Conditions of sale: This book is sold subject to the condition that it shall not, by way of trade or otherwise, be lent, resold, hired out, or otherwise circulated without the publisher's prior consent in any form of binding or cover other than that in which it is published and without a similar condition including this condition being imposed on the subsequent purchaser.

NEL Books are published by
New English Library,
Mill Road, Dunton Green,
Sevenoaks, Kent.
Editorial office: 47 Bedford Square, London WC1B 3DP

Printed and bound in Great Britain by
Richard Clay (The Chaucer Press) Ltd,
Bungay, Suffolk

British Library C.I.P.

Wold, Allen L.
  V: the pursuit of Diana.
  I. Title
  813'.54[F]   PS3573.04/
  ISBN 0–450–5850–6

Chapter 1

Juliet Parrish and Mike Donovan clung together for a long moment. Around them, the huge command center of the Visitors' Los Angeles Mother Ship was nearly silent. Where once thirty or more Visitor technicians worked at their various stations, now only two sat at their posts—Martin, the fifth columnist leader, was at the navigation console, and Barbara, his unofficial second-in-command, was at the communications center. Elias Taylor leaned against the blown-open entrance doors, grinning at his friends, while Elizabeth Maxwell calmly sat by the doomsday device which she alone, with her half-human, half-Visitor powers, had been able to turn off, thus saving the Earth from almost certain destruction.

But for a moment Mike and Julie were not aware of even these few friends. Their need for each other was compounded by the emotional relief of victory, and heightened by the near catastrophe of global destruction. Right now Julie wanted to be alone in some bedroom with Mike, while he, to his own surprise, felt the need for her to comfort him. He had to be the strong one, though, so Julie could continue to be strong. The Visitors were gone, victory was theirs, but there was so much left to do toward putting the world back to rights again.

Over at the entrance, Elias let his gaze wander around the command center. His only concern, once they returned to Earth, was how to fit himself back into society. The thought of returning to his old way of life—to burglary, drug dealing, and petty crime—had no appeal to him anymore. Anger had motivated him before, and frustration, but now he knew that the need for excitement, for thrills had also played a large part in shaping his career, and since he'd joined the rebels he'd had all the excitement anyone could want, enough to last him for the rest of his life. But he wasn't too worried. He knew he wasn't alone anymore. His friends, both human and Visitor, would see him through whatever trials remained.

An opened wall hatch in the bulkhead beyond the doomsday machine seemed somehow significant. He looked again at these few people doing what needed to be done, and thought there should be one more.

"Hey," he said at last, straightening up from his comfortable slouch. "Where's Diana?"

Julie looked at him, and her face lost some of its calm. She disengaged herself from Mike's embrace and nodded at the open hatch. "I let her escape," she said simply.

Mike stepped back and looked down at her in surprise. "But why?" he asked. At their stations, Barbara and Martin paused to look at her uncertainly.

"I didn't want to," Julie said. Her voice carried a silent appeal for understanding. "I'm not really sure what happened. But while I was keeping her covered, it was almost as if part of me were back in the conversion chamber. Diana didn't speak, but I could hear her voice in my head. She kept saying, 'Don't move, be still, it will get you if you move.' My God, she wasn't talking. She was *thinking* at me! I wasn't expecting that. I was expecting her to run or attack or something, but she just sat there in the corner. By the time I realized what was happening, she was halfway through that hatch." She turned to Martin. "What *was* happening?" she asked. "Telepathy?"

"I've never heard of anything like that," Martin said, "but then, I'm not a conversion technician."

"She can't have gotten far," Mike Donovan said. "The toxin must have spread through the whole ship by now."

"Except for here," Barbara pointed out. "There may be other pockets of clean air elsewhere, but that won't matter to Diana. That hatch leads to an escape shuttle. Mike, I don't think Diana's even on the ship anymore."

"Damn," Elias said. Elizabeth continued to sit quietly.

"She still can't get far," Martin said. "We're too far from Earth now. The shuttle will never make it back there before its life support runs out. Those emergency shuttles are designed with very high power but limited range."

"I don't like it," Mike said. "Especially the implication that she had some kind of telepathic control over Julie. Why didn't she try that on someone before?"

"From what Julie's just told us," Barbara said, "it sounds like a by-product of the conversion process, and Julie's the only one of us here who suffered that."

"It was so strange," Julie said. "I wish we could find out more about it."

"We'll have time after we get back home," Mike told her, reaching out for her again. "Right now this is our first order of business."

Martin moved from console to console, reading dials, checking status lights. One particular panel held his attention.

"What is it?" Elias Taylor asked, coming up behind him and looking over his shoulder.

"Damage report," Martin said. "When we tried to get the doomsday device away from Earth, we accelerated too hard and too fast. Two of the engines went down in the attempt, and it looks like the others are failing too." He flipped switches, and the all but imperceptible humming of the drives stopped. "There's been some structural damage as well. These ships aren't designed to move through atmosphere except at a slow coast. We're going to have to make some repairs, or when we get back to Earth we'll just fall like a rock instead of floating over Los Angeles."

"Can you fix it?" Mike Donovan asked.

"Not by myself. It really takes a whole team to fly this thing. That's why we're having trouble now. If I'd had a full crew when we were pulling away from Earth, we probably could have avoided damaging the ship. But it's been a long time since I studied any engineering, and even with help, I'll need some technicians who specialize in engine maintenance."

"How about Willie?" Elias asked. "Or one of the other fifth columnists down in the docking bay?"

"Willie's just a cryogenics worker," Martin said. "Scott might be able to help, but I think we're in big trouble."

"It may not be as bad as it seems," Barbara said, looking up from a large display panel showing a diagram of the ship. "The ship's atmosphere monitor indicates that the toxin didn't spread as far as we'd thought." The others came over to see what she was talking about.

"Each major section of the ship," she said, pointing at the display, "is represented diagrammatically. Here we are, and here are the crew's quarters, recreation area, the water hold, and so on. Each red section is contaminated, but see, that's only this area here." She pointed to the docking bay, the main corridors leading from it to the command center, and a section of cabins or offices off to one side of the main corridors. "Diana must have sealed off most of the ship, probably to keep us bottled up when we made our attack. But it also kept the rest of the ship free of contamination."

"That means most of the crew probably survived," Martin said with obvious relief. "I have to admit I hated the thought of killing everybody like that. After all, most of the crew are only technicians and workers, people who just take orders."

"Then surely some engine technicians have survived," Julie said.

"But can we trust them?" Donovan asked.

"I sure wouldn't," Elias Taylor said. "Think about it, Julie. If they had done to us what we've done to them, would we want to help them?"

"That's a point," Julie said, "but more important is that even if we could trust them, we don't have enough antitoxin on board." She turned to Martin. "If we can find the technicians you need, can we get them to the engines without exposing them to contamination?"

"I don't think so," he answered, examining the display panel. "See, the crew's quarters are here, the engineering section is here, and the only way is through this area, the central access area." That part of the display glowed bright red.

"How many do we need?" Elias asked. "Maggie brought enough antitoxin for thirty to forty people."

"That would be enough," Martin said, "if it hasn't already been used. But how would you get it to them?" The human rebels didn't understand his question, but Barbara did.

"Think about it," she said. "In order to give them the antitoxin, you'll have to unseal a portion of the ship. You can't get in to them otherwise. And if you unseal, the toxin will get to them before you do."

"Goddamn it!" Julie cried. "If it were just us, all right, we've been willing to die for our cause, though to come so close and not quite make it is almost more than I can stand. But there are ten thousand human beings in the holds of this ship. They'll die too if we don't get the ship back to Earth."

"And I'd guess about two thousand of our crew are still alive," Barbara said, "if you figure that most of those who died from the toxin were soldiers and not workers."

"There may be a way out," Martin suggested hesitantly. "The ship carried enough air to recycle three times. If we could get all the rebels and fifth columnists in the contaminated area up here to the command center and somehow seal off the entrance Elias blew, we could open the docking bay and flush the air out of that part of the ship. We'd have to use up a lot of our air reserves to make sure all the toxin was blown out, but if we can effect sufficient repairs to return to Los Angeles, we could pump more air aboard once we were back in Los Angeles's atmosphere."

"But the toxin is all over the city by now," Elias said. "Not counting the smog, the air there wouldn't do you any good."

"The toxin wouldn't have drifted that high up," Mike Donovan reassured him. "At least not yet. Most of the toxin released by the balloons will be in the lower two or three miles of the atmosphere. We could put the ship out beyond the prevailing winds, maybe somewhere in the north Pacific where the air will be clean for at least a year."

"I think it's the only chance we've got," Barbara said. "But if we're going to do it, we'd better get started. With all engines shut down, we don't have power to keep our life support going for long."

"And there're all our friends down in the docking bay,"

Julie said. "God, they must be wondering what's been happening up here."

"I can talk to them from here," Barbara said, going to the master communications panel.

"Even it we flush out all the toxin in the air," Martin said, "we're going to have trouble with the stuff that will be trapped in the clothing of those who died in the corridors."

"Maybe we can move all the bodies into one of these sections," Donovan said, pointing to a red area near the main corridor, "and then seal it off completely."

"Yes, that's possible. And here," Martin pointed to a section of the corridor not far from the command center, "that's a security door, so we can keep the atmosphere in here while the rest of this area is being flushed."

"But wait," Juliet said. "Our people will have the toxin all over their clothes too."

"Nobody said decontamination would be simple," Martin said, "but we've got other uniforms, and we can set up a shower system."

"I've got the docking bay on the screen," Barbara said, and they all turned to see what was going on down there.

William sat beside Harmony Moore's body in one of the compartments of the shuttle.

"Come on," Sancho Gomez said from the door, "there's nothing more you can do."

"I know," William said. His voice was flat, the strange resonance peculiar to the Visitors somehow subdued by his grief. "But I told her I'd never leave her."

"She'll be all right here," Sancho said, coming over to lay a reassuring hand on William's shoulder. "We have wounded friends out there who need our help."

William sighed, then nodded and got to his feet. Leaning on Sancho for support, he went with him out into the docking bay.

The red powder of the toxin stained every surface and hung in the air like a cloud though it was now slowly sifting down to cover the deck with a layer of crimson dust. Rebels and fifth columnists were moving among those of their friends who had fallen to enemy fire. They had taken surprisingly few casualties, but not all were unscathed. The wounded were being made comfortable until some kind of first aid could be brought to them.

Speakers high in the walls came to life. "Attention all rebels and fifth columnists," a female voice said. "This is Barbara. We have taken control of the ship, and the doomsday bomb has been deactivated. But we have more work to do." Quickly she described the situation and the rough plan that had been worked out.

Caleb Taylor and Maggie Blodgett came over to join Sancho and William as they listened to Barbara's report. "I wish I knew if Elias was all right," Caleb said.

"We'll find out soon enough," Maggie reassured him. "Right now we've got to get everybody up to the command center."

"I'll get right on it," Sancho said, and went off to organize litter crews to carry the wounded while William closed the shuttle hatch. With Caleb and Maggie supervising, they soon had all the humans and Visitors in order.

"I don't like this," Caleb said. "How can we trust those engineers Barbara says we need?"

"I don't know," Maggie said, "but I don't think we have any choice." She turned to the others. "All right," she called out, "let's get a move on." Then the speakers came on once more, but the voice was Juliet Parrish's this time.

"Maggie," Julie's voice said, "can you hear me?"

"Yes," Maggie said to the air as the rebels filed past her.

"Good," Julie said. "How much antitoxin is left?"

"I think about ten or fifteen doses. It's on the shuttle."

"Bring it with you," Juliet told her, "and hurry. With our power down, we won't be able to breathe ourselves after a while."

Maggie hurried back to the shuttle and went inside. She had to pass through the compartment where Harmony's body lay in order to get to the pitifully small suppy of antitoxin. She got the pills from their storage place and came back. She couldn't help herself; she had to pause a moment with Harmony.

"We knew each other for so short a time," she said softly. She wiped a red smear from the now cold face. "But you didn't die in vain—I hope." Then she hurried out to follow the others.

The scene at Visitor Headquarters in Los Angeles was doubly chaotic. Bodies of Visitor soldiers littered the ground, mingled with those of the few rebels who had fallen. A thin red haze hung like a pall at knee height, slowly dissipating across the grounds. At the same time, the rebels who had discovered the cache of champagne and other fine beverages that Steven, the Visitor security chief, had kept on hand for his human collaborators, were having a wild, impromptu party. Even the wounded were joining in.

But not Robert Maxwell. He and a few other rebels were checking the bodies of their fallen companions, finding those who still lived and carrying them to one of the trucks. Robert was anxious to get back to the lighthouse rebel base, concerned for those who were still there, and especially his three daughters. Robin, he knew, would be a particular problem, at least until Elizabeth, his half-human granddaughter, was returned safely—if she ever was. And there was a lot of work still ahead of them all putting their lives back together.

Inside, in Steven's control room, several rebels stood examining the wall of computers, communicators, and other equipment the Visitors had installed. Steven's body had been unceremoniously pushed to one side. Jason Cunningham, a tall slender man in his late forties, went from panel to panel, examining the dials, the readouts, the controls and displays.

"We've got to keep this from being destroyed," he told his two companions. "If we can figure out how all this stuff works, we my gain something from the Visitors after all."

"You're the electrical engineer," Ian Browne said. Not as tall as Jason, he was even more slender, and rapidly balding in spite of not yet being thirty. "All I know is how to fix TV sets."

"Then you know enough not to damage anything while we take this apart," Jason told him.

"Can't we leave it until later?" Markos Dimitrios asked. The shortest of the three, his Greek features were darkly handsome. "I want to go out and join the party."

"If we don't do something to protect this equipment," Jason said, "it will be destroyed by vandals. You saw how eager the others were to rip it apart. People won't want anything of the Visitors' to survive, so either we set a guard or try to take as much as we can with us."

"Well, I'm not going to stay here any longer than I have to," Ian said. "I've got to get back to my TV store and find out if my family's okay."

"Then let's get to work," Jason said. "We'll need screwdrivers, wire cutters, and wrenches." He turned to Markos. "You said there was a shop of some kind in the basement, didn't you?"

"Right. I'll go get whatever I can find."

"Great. Now, Ian," Jason said as Markos hurried off, "some of these devices just slip into mounts. Be careful with the plugs and stack everything over on that table. When Markos comes back, you show him what to do. I've got to get a truck and some help in carrying this stuff out." He left the man to his task and went out onto the balcony.

Jason went over to the stone railing, where the body of Mike's mother, Eleanor Dupres, still lay, a look of surprise on her face. Below him he could see none of the rebel leaders. Only revelers were visible. He called down to one.

"Find Robert Maxwell," he said. "I need some help up here."

"Haven't seen him," the man called back, his voice thick with drink.

"Then get Ham Tyler," Jason said.

"Haven't seen him either."

"Well, go *looking* for him, man," Jason Cunningham said as he hurried toward the stairs. "You," he called out to another rebel who was talking with two women. "Can you back a truck up here?"

"Sure thing," the man said and trotted off.

"What's up?" one of the women asked.

"We're going to save some Visitor technology," Jason told her. "They left a lot of stuff up here, and I'm going to need help getting it out." He started back to the control room, the two women coming up the stairs behind him.

Inside he found Markos and Ian working at disassembling

the mass of electronics. Two dozen or more devices were already stacked on the table by the door, their wires dangling and tangled. Each piece of equipment was only two inches thick, typical of the compactness of Visitor electronics.

"It comes apart easily," Ian said, wielding a screwdriver to disconnect a heavy cable from a conduit, "but there's an awful lot of it."

"Cut the wires if you have to," Jason said, then turned to the two women. "Get this down to the truck," he said. "Be careful with it if you can, but speed is more important than caution if it comes to that." He turned back to the instrument wall, picked up a wrench, and started undoing some of the more substantial mountings. "Going to be a real jigsaw puzzle putting this back together again," he said.

"What do you want?" a man's voice came from the door. Jason turned to see Ham Tyler, nicknamed the Fixer, and behind him the bulk of his friend, Chris Faber.

"Something here you might be interested in," Jason said, "if we can ever figure out how it works. I think some of this equipment was used for surveillance and espionage."

Ham's interest was suddenly aroused, though his only action was to raise an eyebrow. "Not really my line," he said, "but you've got a good point. Clemmons will know what to do with this. I'll send a message to him over in Detroit."

"Great," Cunningham said, and went back to his work.

Ham and Chris stepped out of the way as the two women rebels came back for another load of equipment, then went back out onto the balcony.

"I think we've done just about all we can here," Ham said. Chris Faber nodded, and again they stepped aside as the women, their arms laden with electronics, went past them down the stairs to where the truck was parked. The Fixer and his colleague followed, ducked around the open tailgate, and started across the lawn. Here the party was finally beginning to wind down. They saw Robert Maxwell, who now had drunks as well as wounded to attend to, and went over to say good-bye.

"But you can't leave now," Maxwell said. "I can't lead all these people by myself."

"You seem to be doing a pretty good job," Ham said.

"At least stick around until Mike and Julie get back," Robert pleaded. "You're the only other authority figure we have."

"My job's finished once the battle is over," Ham Tyler said. "You're the one who's going to have to put the pieces back together again."

"I *would* kind of like to see Alice again," Chris said musingly.

"Who's Alice?" Ham asked.

"Just a friend," Chris replied. "Just like to say good-bye."

"You're getting soft," Ham said disgustedly.

Robert grinned. "I thought you and Alice seemed to be getting on pretty well ever since the raid on the pumping station."

"She's a tough lady," Chris Faber said, his face bland.

"So, how about it," Robert asked Ham, "you going to stay with us just a little while longer?"

"I guess I've got no choice." He rubbed his hand across his thinning hair. "And, yes," he admitted, "I would like to know if Donovan's all right."

"That's what's got me worried," Maxwell said. "We should have heard from him by now."

"At least we know that they were able to stop the doomsday bomb," Chris said.

"Unless it blew up on the other side of the world," Ham countered.

"No," Robert said. "A bomb that big would have been noticeable even then, if it had gone off. Even against the full light of day, we would have seen the flash shining around the world like a new kind of sunset. But the fact that it didn't go off is *all* we know."

"All right," the Fixer said, "I'll go along with you, but there are other groups all across the country, and they're going to have to be informed too. If we don't hear from Donovan pretty soon, I'll just have to get back to the network. Besides, there will be plenty of other jobs for me during the aftermath."

"Right now," Robert Maxwell said, "we've got to get everybody into the trucks, and a lot of them are drunk. They'll follow your orders, Ham. Let's do it."

"There's one other thing," Ham said. "If Donovan and the

others *are* all okay, they'll be bringing that Mother Ship back, isn't that right?"

"Of course," Robert answered, "unless they want to stay up there forever."

"How do you think the people of Los Angeles are going to feel about it when that thing is back in the sky again?"

"I hadn't thought about that," Robert said.

William and another fifth columnist, George, stepped out of a large compartment into a corridor of the ship. Both carried sidearms, as did two or three others who, having been given the antitoxin, were at least momentarily immune to the thick red dust which covered everything. Other Visitors, trustees wearing respirators and torn-off sleeves to distinguish them from fifth columnists, were carrying bodies from the corridor into the compartment. These workers were a few of the survivors whom William had known, and had suggested could be trusted, at least somewhat. Those fifth columnists who did not need respirators were removing all weapons to yet another compartment before the trustees got to them.

"It hurts to find people you recognize," George said, turning over one of the dead soldiers.

"Are you sure that compartment can be completely sealed?" William asked, indicating the place to which the bodies were being removed.

"I checked all the inside vents," George said. He moved to another body and tossed the dead soldier's rifle to a fifth columnist. Only those who had been with the invasion force were trusted to handle weapons, and there were few enough of them.

William went up the corridor in the direction of the docking bay. The bodies here had all been taken to another compartment, which also had been sealed. Two or three of his shipmates, now in respirators, were sitting on the deck, resting a moment before going back to work.

"Is it my imagination," one of these asked, "or is the air beginning to get bad in here?" He was breathing heavily, and not just from the exertion. The temperature was slowly rising as well.

"The ventilation has been cut off for over an hour," William said. "Nobody gets fresh air until this corridor is cleared." He didn't like playing the tough guard, but somebody had to do the job. The three in respirators struggled to their feet and went back up the corridor to where George and the other fifth columnists were supervising the continuing work. William sighed and followed them. There was an awful lot to do, and so little time to do it in.

Elias Taylor stood guard just inside the door to the quarters that so recently had been Diana's. A rebel and a fifth columnist, escorting three Visitors in respirators, came to a halt until Taylor let them in. There at a table sat Martin and Peter, shuffling a stack of papers. Peter, a fifth columnist of long standing, checked names off a list while Martin took three slim folders from a stack beside him.

The Visitors and their guards stopped in front of the table. At Martin's nod, Elias closed the portal. There came the sound of air hissing through the ventilator system. After a moment, that too stopped.

"You can take off your respirators now," Peter told the three prisoners. The two men hesitated, but the third, a woman, complied immediately. When she didn't collapse choking, the other two followed suit.

"The situation is this," Martin said. "We are stranded in space. All the other Mother Ships are now on their way out of the solar system. At this moment, we can neither join them nor go back to Earth. In trying to get Diana's doomsday device as far from the planet as possible, we suffered the loss of two engines and some slight structural damage. That must be repaired." He looked down at his folders. "You were all with the engineering section. Are you willing to help us get this ship running again?"

One Visitor, whose artificial face had Oriental features, shrugged his shoulders. "I couldn't even if I wanted to," he said. "I was just a maintenance man, not an engineer."

"How about you?" Peter asked the second man. The prisoner just stared at him, disdain evident on his face. Peter sighed and made a mark on his list. Then he and Martin both looked at the woman. Her gaze shifted from one to the other. She put her hands to her face a moment, then sighed.

"Yes," she said, "I'll help. I guess we'll all die if I don't."

"That's correct," Martin said.

Elias came up and led the woman Visitor through a door at the side while the guards gave the two men their respirators back. One of them picked up the third respirator to take with them back to the other Visitors yet to be interviewed. Elias returned, let the four of them out of the room, then turned back to Martin.

"How many so far?" he asked.

"Seven," Martin said. The strain was showing. "But none of them is really qualified. And we're not going to be able to keep refreshing the air in here much longer."

Elias heard footsteps out in the corridor and went to admit three more prisoners and their two guards. As before, the prisoners were wearing respirators. And as before, once they were inside, Elias closed the door so the air could be refreshed.

Martin took up another stack of three folders, having put the last three to one side. Facing him now were three women, one apparently black. Once again he briefly told them the situation and asked if they would help. The three women looked at him but didn't answer.

"You all know," Peter said, "that Our Leader lied to us. The inhabitants of this world are not animals, but people not that different from ourselves in many ways. We have committed a great crime by trying to steal their water and take them back as food. It is up to us to make some small restitution."

"I'd rather die," the black Visitor said. She turned her face away. The second woman looked at her with disgust.

"We may die anyway," she said. "Much good it will do you. Yes," she said to Peter, "I'll help."

"You're a fool," the third woman said. "How long do you think they'll let you live after they get you back to Earth?"

"I'll take my chances," the second woman said.

"Thank you," Martin told her as Elias came up to lead her to the inner room. The guards gave the other two prisoners their respirators and, carrying the third respirator, led them back out into the hall.

"That one will be a real help," Peter said, checking a name off his list. "She's a qualified engineering supervisor."

"I don't think I trust her," Elias Taylor said. "She seemed just a little too willing."

"I don't think so," Martin said, "but even so, what choice do we have?"

"I know, I know," Elias said, "but think about it. She could sabotage the engines instead of repairing them."

"I think I can remember enough of my training," Martin said, "to be able to detect that if she tries it." The door tone sounded, signaling the arrival of yet more interviewees. "Let's get back to work," Martin said tiredly.

Elias started to protest, then shook his head and went to open the door. Beyond, as expected, were two more guards and three more Visitors. This was going to take a long time.

Barbara sat at the communications console in the command center. The screen in front of her showed the interior of a barracks. Twenty or so Visitor soldiers, armed and armored but with their helmets off, sat or stood around within range of the camera.

"Let me speak to your ranking officer," Barbara said. The soldiers, grim and angry, exchanged glances until one, a sergeant, came to the front of the group.

"I guess that's me," he said. His attitude indicated he didn't really give a damn.

"Sergeant," Barbara said in a tired voice, "as you are now aware, we control the entire ship. You are the last platoon of soldiers left alive. The others all died when the toxin was pumped into portions of the ventilating system." The sergeant lost his devil-may-care expression, and the other soldiers with him began muttering to each other. "That is hard news, I know," Barbara went on, "but that's the way it is."

"So what do you want?" the sergeant asked.

"We don't want to kill any more of you than is necessary," Barbara said, "but we can't let you keep your weapons. Several of our people are outside your door right now. Put all your weapons into the security locker and move to the far side of the room. I'll unseal the door then, and let our people in."

"And then they'll shoot us all down?" a soldier in back called out.

"No," Barbara said. "If we wanted to kill you we could do it without risk. All I'd have to do is pump toxin directly into your barracks." She didn't like threatening them with this, especially since she knew several of the men and women there. The sergeant's expression became even more grim. Barbara let the soldiers talk it over among themselves.

"What will it be?" Barbara asked after a moment. "You'll have to make up your minds fast. We have too much else to do."

The sergeant came away from his men and again faced the camera. "All right," he said. "We'll go along with you."

Barbara watched as one by one the soldiers went to the locker at the side of the barracks, put in his or her weapon, and then retreated to the other side of the room. She tried to see that each did as instructed, but sometimes two or three of the soldiers would crowd in together. At last they finished. Barbara took a breath, punched a button, and the barracks portal unsealed.

Outside the portal, two rebels and two fifth columnists heard the lock click, then went inside, guns drawn. While one of the fifth columnists went to the gun cabinet, the other three kept the soldiers covered. The fifth columnist at the cabinet took a heavy device the size of a paperback book from his pocket and placed it over the latch. But before he could trip the lock, one of the soldiers pulled a pistol he'd kept concealed, and shot him through the head.

His victory was short-lived. The other three guards all fired in unison, and the soldier fell, blue sparks racing across his chest and abdomen.

"Anybody else want to try something?" the rebel in charge asked while the other fifth columnist went over to the gun cabinet. The soldiers stood silently.

"He's dead," the man at the cabinet said, kneeling over his fallen companion. He stood and touched the switch on the locking device. There was a crackling as bolts welded themselves to the latch and door. He grabbed his dead friend by the shoulders and while the two rebels covered him, dragged him out the door.

"You'll have to tend to your own dead yourself," the rebel in charge said. As he stepped back out into the hall, the door closed, and he could hear it lock again.

Barbara watched the scene grimly. Several of the soldiers went to the cabinet, but the locking device resisted their efforts to remove it.

"There's still one gun in that room," Mike Donovan said, coming up to look over her shoulder.

"That's true, but the situation is a lot better than it was before. We could have lost twenty lives instead of just two."

"But we can't trust any of them," Mike said. "Can the gun shoot off the lock?"

"No. It's a special security device designed against that very thing. At least we can stop worrying about them for a while."

She switched the view to another part of the ship, a section of corridor where the fighting had been heavy. It was clear of bodies now, and the red dust on the floor was smeared with footprints and the tracks of dragged corpses.

"Looks good," Mike said. "How much more left to go?"

Barbara switched the scene again. Another empty corridor. Yet another shot showed Sancho Gomez and his crew still working. Visitor trustees in respirators were carrying bodies into a compartment under the watchful eye of several armed rebels and fifth columnists.

Barbara turned on the mike and spoke into it. "How is it going?" she asked.

Sancho Gomez looked up at the corner of the corridor wall from which Barbara's words had come.

"We're almost through here," he told her. "Then just two more sections left."

"Very good," he heard her answer as he went back to his work.

The compartment into which the bodies were being carried was stacked high. Trustees in respirators brought in the last of them from the corridor, then left as Sancho surveyed the scene one more time. He turned away at last and closed the door behind him. He did not notice that one of the last bodies, that of Captain Jake, did not lie perfectly still but rolled over.

"That's the last of them," Elias Taylor said as he let yet another group of guards and prisoners into Diana's quarters. Martin and Peter slumped in their chairs as the three approached their desk. The prisoners were all men this time, all resembling Caucasians.

The resonance in Peter's voice was coarsened by fatigue as he explained yet again what he wanted of these people. One of the three men nodded his head in agreement.

"We could have learned a lot from humans," he said. "Not all their technology is behind ours. I saw some articles on recombinant DNA. We haven't come nearly as far in that area. I'll be more than glad to help."

"They're just *relavish*," the one beside him said, spitting a stream of venom onto the floor in front of the desk. "You don't expect me to associate with creatures like that."

"What does *relavish* mean?" Elias asked from the door.

"Mammalian vermin," Martin translated, "sort of like rats, in your language, but inedible."

"But they're not inedible," the third prisoner said. "Humans are very tasty. Will we be able to keep the ones we've got in the hold?"

"No," Martin said shortly, and gestured to the guards. Elias came to lead the one who had agreed to cooperate to the back room to join the other Visitor technicians who had similarly expressed a willingness to help. The other two were given their respirators. Elias came back to let them out with their guards. At the same time he let in Juliet Parrish and Caleb Taylor, his father.

"How's it going, Pop?" Elias asked.

"We've got the corridors cleared," Caleb said. "We can start flushing the air any time now."

"Good," Juliet said. "How many technicians do we have?" she asked the two fifth columnists behind the desk.

Peter looked at his list. "Seventeen," he said, "and several of them are even qualified."

"They'll all have to work under armed guard, though," Martin cautioned. "I don't know any of them personally, and we can't take a chance on trusting them."

"I agree," Caleb said. "I'm going to personally pick their guards, and if any one of them even looks like he's trying to sabotage the engines, he'll finish the job in a wheelchair."

The communicator at the side of the desk suddenly chimed. Martin pressed a button. "Yes," he said, "what is it?"

"Is Julie there?" Barbara's voice asked.

"Right here," Juliet said.

"You'd better come up to the command center right away," Barbara said. "We're getting a signal, a strong one, from somewhere between here and your moon."

Mike and Barbara were sitting at the communications console, listening to a loud, strange, almost musically modulated signal.

"What *is* that," Mike Donovan asked, "a Visitor version of heavy-metal rock?"

"No," Barbara said as Juliet and Martin came in. "It's a distress call."

"But who could be sending it?" Julie asked.

"There's only one person I can think of," Martin said, "and that's Diana."

"He's right," Barbara agreed. "And only an escape shuttle has a transmitter powerful enough to send a signal that strong."

"And as far as we know," Donovan said, "there are no other escape shuttles out there, so it has to be Diana." Martin nodded. "Can you tell what she's saying?"

Barbara punched buttons on the console. "I'm afraid not," she said. "It sounds like a standard code, but the computer can't translate it."

"Then it's not just a call for help," Martin said. "That would be broadcast in the clear." He reached over Barbara's shoulder and touched a few more buttons. "No good," he went on. "That's a high security signal, for ship's commanders only."

"But who can she be calling?" Juliet asked. "Can that signal reach all the way to Sirius?"

"No," Barbara answered. "It can't even get to the rest of the fleet. They're all well out of range by now."

"Take a fix on it," Mike told her. "Once we get this ship running again, I want to go pick her up. She has a lot to answer for."

Barbara bent over the console. "It's like I said," she told them. "It's coming from a place about a quarter of the way between here and your moon. But it's going toward the *moon*, not Earth."

Chapter 2

The sun was setting over a calm Pacific Ocean as the rebel trucks pulled into their lighthouse base. Robert Maxwell was among the first to jump out of the back of the lead truck, eager to see to the welfare of his children. A woman on guard at the base of the lighthouse shouted a greeting to them and disappeared inside. Before Robert could get to the door, Robin, his eldest daughter, came running out to meet him. She threw herself into her father's arms.

"Oh, Father," she cried, "we were so worried." He swung her around once and put her down.

"We had a few casualties," he told her gently, "but we won. Steven is dead, the Visitor Headquarters is empty." Behind him, other trucks were stopping, and other rebels were helping the wounded out. "How are Polly and Katie?" he asked.

Robin watched with growing concern as rebels helped their friends toward the building that served as their hospital. "They're inside," she said. "So many wounded?"

"Most of them are just hung over," Robert said, laughing. He put his arm around his daughter and went into the lighthouse. He barely got in the door when Polly and Katie came running up. He grabbed them both, laughing and weeping at the same time.

"Is it really all over," Polly asked when she could speak again.

"I think so," Robert said. "I surely hope so."

"Except," Ham Tyler said from behind him, "for putting the world back together again." He turned to Maxwell. "Some of our people confiscated all the electronics from Visitor Headquarters. We'll need a place to set it up."

"We've got some room in the garage next door," a woman rebel with long, dark hair said. It was Alice Reynolds. "Is Chris all right?"

"I am now," Chris Faber said, coming in through the door. For a man of his bulk, he moved with surprising speed and grace. He enveloped Alice in an enthusiastic embrace, and then went back out with her to supervise the handling of the Visitor equipment.

"I think everything's going to be all right," Robert said to his daughters.

"Except for Elizabeth," Robin said. "We haven't heard a word from the Mother Ship."

"Nothing at all?" Robert asked.

"No, Father. Linda's been scanning all the possible channels."

"Where is she now?" Robert asked.

"We've got everything set up on the second floor," Robin said, and went with him as he mounted the central stairs.

Linda McReady sat among a clutter of radio equipment, some of it of earthly manufacture, some of it captured Visitor devices. Several speakers emitted voices, their volumes turned down, each set to a different channel, while at the same time Linda listened to a single earphone clipped over her head. She set the tuner to one wavelength, listened a moment, then turned the dial slightly. Several tape recorders were going beside her, picking up the broadcasts received from other tuners. She looked up as Robert and Robin Maxwell entered her cluttered office.

"Any word at all from Donovan?" Robert asked.

"I'm sorry," Linda said. "Of course, with only a skeleton crew here, I might have missed something. You can play back the tapes if you like."

"They can't all be dead," Robin said. "Elizabeth is still up there with them."

"I know, Binna," her father said, "but all we know for sure is that the ship left along with the others. It could be on its way to Sirius by now."

"Oh, Father, don't say that."

"I know it's not easy to accept," Robert said, "but you have to be prepared for the worst."

"What I'm worried about," Linda said, "is all those people the Visitors had stored in the hold. Elizabeth is half Visitor, Robin, but to the aliens the others are just cattle, to be slaughtered and eaten."

Alice Reynolds and another rebel came in at that moment.

"Linda," Alice said, "let Joseph take over for a while. Come and see what we've got."

Linda took off her earphone and handed it to the young man with Alice. "What is it?" she asked.

"All the equipment from Visitor Headquarters," Alice told her.

"Holy shit," Linda said, "this I've got to see." She started to the door, then turned back to Robert and Robin. "Come on," she said. "If anything can make contact with Mike and Julie, this stuff should." They all hurried out, leaving Joseph to tend the tuners.

Benches were crowded with pieces of Visitor electronics. The far wall of the garage had been cleared, and there a makeshift set of racks was being constructed to hold it all. Jason Cunningham was supervising the construction, while Ian Browne and Markos Dimitrios directed other rebels who were bringing in yet more. Linda, Alice, Robert, and Robin came over to watch.

"Are you responsible for this?" Robert Maxwell asked Jason.

"I couldn't leave it behind," Jason said half defensively.

"It's terrific," Robert said "I didn't even know it was there."

Chris Faber came in, carrying a particularly large device which consisted of a flat screen and a set of knobs. Ian showed him where to put it while Markos and two women pulled up another bench.

"I know what that is," Linda McReady said, pointing to one of the pieces of electronics. "I've got one just like it upstairs, but it's broken."

"A communicator?" Alice asked as Jason Cunningham turned to listen in.

"Right. But there are a couple other components that should be hooked up to it."

"Yes," Jason said. "You're right, there were." He looked over the chaos on the benches. "There's one," he said, pointing, and Linda went to it. "I'll show you how it was connected. I took that one apart myself."

"This one too," Ian Browne said, holding out something the size of a cassette player. There were no controls, only a horse's tail of colored wires sprouting from the back.

"This is fantastic," Robert Maxwell said. "How soon do you think you can get it working?"

"Ten or fifteen minutes, maybe," Linda answered. "This is obviously first priority."

"You've got it," said Robert. "Because, look, if Donovan and Julie *are* all right, if they *do* bring the ship back, we're going to have a real problem on our hands. Those ten thousand human beings in the ship's hold will have to be brought back down to Earth and reprocessed."

"That's right," Linda said, "and the only place they can do that is the plant north of Pomona, where the Visitors were putting those people into suspended animation in the first place."

"So, what I figure," Robert Maxwell said, "is that that's where Donovan and Julie will come down—assuming of course that they're still alive." He turned and grabbed Chris, who had just brought in another piece of equipment that looked like a cross between a video game and an old-fashioned radio.

"Where's Ham?" he asked. "We're going to have to get out to the suspension plant."

"He's at the infirmary," Chris said. "I'll tell him. We'll be ready to move out in an hour."

"But we can't leave here," Robin said. "What if they call us from the ship?"

"We won't all be going," Linda said. "I'll be staying here to work with the electronics. You think I'm going to let this stuff just sit?"

"Me too," Jason Cunningham said. "We've got a gold mine here, and if I can figure out how even one percent of it works, we'll revolutionize the communications industry. And besides, there are the children. We'll need some people to look after them."

"All right," Robin said, "but if Mike lands at the suspension plant, I want to be there."

"No," her father told her. "We don't know how many Visitors might still be there. We may have to fight to take the place."

"But the toxin," Robin wailed. "Won't that have killed them all?"

"It will eventually, but there isn't that much in the air, and the wind direction has been away from the plant all day. I'm sorry, Binna, but if we have to fight again, I don't want you there."

"We'll keep in touch," Alice Reynolds reassured her, looking up from something with a keyboard. She went over to another bench at the side and picked up a standard army-issue radio. "Channel fourteen," she said as she handed it to Robert. "Either Joseph or I will be listening at all times."

"Oh, Father," Robin said, "I wish you didn't have to go out again."

"So do I, sweetheart, but this won't be like the last time. You can help out by spelling Linda on the radio now and then."

"I will," Robin said.

Chris Faber came back in. "We're ready to roll," he said. "At least those of us who didn't overindulge back at Visitor Headquarters."

"I'll call you as soon as I get there," Robert said to Linda as he held up the army radio. Then he joined Chris, who cast a longing glance at Alice before they both left for the trucks.

Linda McReady, Alice Reynolds, and Jason Cunningham sat in front of the jury-rigged wall of alien devices. Ian Browne and Markos Dimitrios were fitting the last of them in place, though there were still hundreds of wires hanging out. Unlike the installation at Visitor Headquarters, there was plenty of space between each device to allow the rebels to make connections as they figured things out.

"I'm not sure where most of this goes," Jason said. "If I'd had time, I'd have drawn a diagram and labeled each piece, but as it is, all I can do is guess. At least we know that everything once fit together in an unbroken mosaic, without the large gaps we have now. Maybe between us we can eventually get it all put back together the way it was."

"Even if we can't," Alice said, "we know which parts belong to the communicator." She turned to another rebel who had just come up. "How's the power, Wilma?" she asked.

"We're all set," Wilma Corrigan answered. "We had to install a few new fuse boxes, but I think we can handle the load."

"Great." Alice turned back to the racks of electronics. "Let that other stuff go," she told Browne and Dimitrios. "I want to see if the communicator works."

Markos stepped aside while Ian tightened one more screw.

"That should do it," Ian said. He went over to an improvised switch box fastened to a side wall. "Let's hope we don't blow everything out on the first try." He pulled the master switch, and here and there among the equipment lights started coming on.

"Nothing exploded," Linda McReady said, "and the communicator seems to be working." She got up from her chair and with Jason Cunningham at her side, started fiddling with the controls. Speakers set on benches nearby started emitting hisses, then clicks, then whistles and moans.

"So far so good," Jason said. "Let's cut out anything we don't need at the moment." He went along one side and Alice the other. Hesitantly at first but gradually with more confidence, each turned off as much of the equipment as he or she could. Linda kept on fiddling with the knobs until suddenly a loud, strange, almost musically modulated signal burst forth from the speakers. Hastily she reach for a large dial and turned the gain down.

"What in hell is that?" Ian Browne asked.

"Nothing of ours," Linda said, "so it must be from the Mother Ship."

"It sounds like some kind of code," Markos said. "Would Julie be broadcasting in code?"

"Not this kind of code," Alice answered. She stepped away from the electronics wall and brought up a wheeled cart. On it were tape recorders and a small computer. She connected cables from the cart to the electronics wall. "We'll record everything and see if the computer can make any sense out of it," she explained, "but I suspect what we have is a Visitor signal of some kind."

"That means Mike and Julie were only partially successful," Ian said.

They heard a gasp from the shadows. "No," Robin said as she came out into the light, "that can't be."

"You shouldn't be here," Alice said, going to comfort her. "Besides, we really don't know what that signal means."

"Can you call them?" Robin asked. "Can you send back and ask?"

"I don't know," Linda McReady said, "but we sure as hell are going to try." She picked up a microphone and plugged the cord into the communicator while Alice Reynolds started the recorders going.

"This is rebel base," Linda said into the mike. "Come in, Mike Donovan. Come in, Juliet Parrish." Alice started typing at the computer's console. The sound of the strange musical signal continued unchanged. Linda fiddled with her dials. "Come in," she called again, but there was no answer.

In the bowels of the Mother Ship, engines of incomprehensible design, gleaming crystal, bright chrome, and dead black hung in a space far larger than the Astrodome. Catwalks, mere spiderwebs by comparison, ran from one pendant machine to another, connecting the bulges, fins, spines, and coils. In the center of the web was a platform hundreds of feet above the shadowed deck. Thirty feet in diameter, it held consoles, panels, and banks of lights which were now all dark. In the center, Caleb Taylor, Sancho Gomez, and the fifth columnist William stood with drawn weapons while six of the Visitor trustee technicians, each with a fifth columnist supervisor, inspected the equipment.

At one point a front panel had been removed, and the technician had inserted a long, silvery probe into the innards, reading the dials on the end he held. At another place a technician had connected wires to circuit buses, which in turn were connected to a hand-held meter. Elsewhere, other technicians were testing, probing, reading, trying to find out what had gone wrong and how to fix it.

Sancho kept fingering his rifle. "It makes me nervous," he said. "They could blow up this whole ship."

"No way," Caleb said. "If they were that sloppy, some careless technician would have done it long ago."

"That's right," William agreed. "I don't know how the engines work, but all our equipment has safeguards built in, just like at the cryogenic plants on Earth."

"That's not exactly reassuring," Caleb said, remembering the accident from which William had saved him.

"I know these people," William said, "at least some of them. They're like me, not like Diana. And anyway, if they really wanted to kill us, all they'd have to do is nothing."

"Or else," Sancho said, "fix it so the engines *couldn't* be repaired."

"That's why we've got people we can trust looking over their shoulders," Caleb Taylor said. Still, he was nervous too. He went up to one of the fifth columnists who was supervising a woman trustee. The technician had opened up a control panel, swinging it to one side like a door, and was holding a large computerlike device in front of it. No wires or probes connected her sensor with the inner workings, but the screen of the device showed changing alien symbols.

"How's it going, Scott?" Caleb asked her fifth columnist guard.

"It's not as bad as it might be," Scott answered. "Acceleration through your atmosphere simply caused excessive vibration, resulting in an electrothermal conduction which degaussed the gravity coils. Nothing has shorted, fortunately, though the lambda alignment is way off and polarity has reversed in several condensors."

"Great. Now, what exactly does that mean?"

"It means we don't have to use any replacement parts but can just retune the circuits."

"Thanks. So how long do you think that will take?"

"Just a couple of hours. First we have to isolate the faulty input channels and redirect the oscillator bus. We can't shut the whole thing down, which would be easier, or we'd lose power altogether."

"And what would that do?"

"All the lights would go out and suffocation would follow within fifteen minutes."

"No, we don't want to do that. But tell me, if you know that much about it, how come you're not doing it yourself?"

"Have you ever rebored the engine in your own car?"

"I get the point. Okay, but is there any way one of these technicians could blow up the ship with what they're doing?"

"Not at all. The worst that could happen would be to permanently disable the two engines we're working on."

"Thanks for the reassurance," Caleb said dryly.

"You needn't worry," Scott told him. "None of these people want to die, and they're not political fanatics."

"I'll have to take your word for it," Caleb Taylor said and went back to rejoin his friends. "Scott's got everything under control," he told them, and wiped the sweat off his forehead.

Juliet Parrish and Mike Donovan sat in the command center, holding hands, watching while Martin directed fifth columnists and other trustee technicians working at various control consoles. The process of flushing the contaminated atmosphere out of the ship was well under way, and only a few areas of the ship's atmospheric display panel were still red. Among those, of course, were the compartments in which the bodies of the Visitor soldiers had been temporarily stored.

Over at the communications console, Barbara was still trying to decode the signal coming from Diana's escape shuttle. Mike, tired of doing nothing, left Juliet and went over to ask Barbara how it was going.

"No luck so far," Barbara told him, "and I don't really expect to break it. It's a code like your public key code, based on very large prime numbers, a million digits long at least."

"Then breaking the code is impossible," Donovan said. "It would take more years than the universe has already existed to try all the possible factors."

"That's true, but it turns out there's an algorithm that can test at least for the range of the primes. Given ten years or so, I think we could break it. The real security lies in changing the code once a year."

"That doesn't really leave us much better off. Can you tell at least where the signal is coming from?"

"The signal source is still moving toward the moon, but remember, while the escape shuttle has lots of power, it won't last long. She's turned off her engines and is coasting now."

Meanwhile, Juliet had gone over to see how Martin was progressing in flushing out the contaminated atmosphere.

"Another hour or so should do it," he told her.

"What about the compartments where the bodies are stored?" Julie asked.

"We'll have to manually rig special exhaust ducts," he said, "but we don't have to worry about them now, at least as far as the toxin is concerned. The real problem will be that the bodies will have begun to decay by the time we get to them. That will be a real mess."

Barbara, at her console, looked up at them. "We can't just leave them there forever," she said.

"What do you do with your dead?" Mike asked her. "You don't eat them, do you?"

"No," Barbara answered, "we're not cannibals, though we may seem like that to you. We bury our dead." She looked at him with silent pleading. "Can we do that when we get back?"

"Of course," Juliet said, coming over to her. "I guess it's been hard for us to realize that you've lost friends too."

"Having to fight your own kind is not easy," Barbara said.

"No, it isn't," Mike Donovan said. "Those kinds of wars can be the worst. Our country had its Civil War, with brother fighting brother, not just friend against friend. The scars remain even after more than a century."

"Wait a minute," Barbara said, turning back to the console. There was a subtle but distinct difference in the signal. "I think someone is trying to get through to us on the same wavelength."

"You're right," Julie said. "That sounds like a voice, but the code signal is so strong I can't make out what they're saying."

Barbara turned up the volume, but the code signal became louder too, and the second signal was so weak that the words, whatever they were, were completely obscured.

"I think it's in English," Donovan said uncertainly.

"Yes," Julie said. "Let me listen." Her face showed the effort of her concentration. "Or maybe it's Dutch," she said, "or German. Can't you do anything to bring it in clearer?" she asked Barbara.

"I'm trying," Barbara said, delicately touching the dials. "It's no good. If it were even a few cycles different, I could filter the code out, but it's on exactly the same wavelength."

"It has to be somebody back at the base," Mike said. "That means they're receiving the code signal too. We have to try to get in touch with them to let them know we're all right."

"I'll try," Barbara said, and bent over her controls.

"What's going on?" Elias Taylor asked, coming up to where Juliet Parrish and Mike Donovan were standing as they watched Barbara trying to get a message through.

"I think our base is trying to contact us," Donovan said, "but Diana's code signal is drowning them out."

"I wish we knew what was going on," Juliet said. "We don't even know if the balloons were successful in spreading the toxin."

"I'm not worried about that," Elias said. "Ham Tyler may be a purebred son of a bitch, but he was in charge of the balloons, and he knows what he's doing." Mike Donovan nodded agreement. "It's what's happened to the rest of the country that I'm concerned about," Elias went on. "I mean, from what I saw happening down there, if I wanted to go back to my old trade, I could make a fortune. Black market, dope, you name it. But I've kind of lost the taste for that kind of thing. What am I going to do for a living after this is all over?"

"I guess we haven't had much time to think about that," Donovan agreed. "But you're right. The most important and powerful people in government, both state and federal, were converted by the Visitors. How are they going to behave without the Visitors to control them?"

"My god, Mike," Julie said, "you're right. And those who couldn't be converted are somewhere on this ship, down in the storage holds."

"But worse," Elias said, "the people back home don't *know* that their President, their senators and governors are Visitor puppets with their strings cut. They'll think, now that the Visitors are gone everything's back to normal."

"The shooting may be over," Mike said grimly, "but the war isn't even half won."

The sudden silence in the command center caught everybody's attention.

"What happened?" Elias Taylor asked, speaking for them all.

"Diana's signal has stopped," Barbara said. "The escape shuttle must have used up its limited power."

"Unless Diana was rescued," Mike suggested.

"By whom?" Julie asked. "All the other ships have gone back to Sirius."

"As far as we know," Barbara cautioned. She turned to another set of instruments. "A Mother Ship," she said after a moment, "is big enough that we could detect it from here if it were anywhere near Diana's escape shuttle, but there's nothing out there, so Diana can't have been rescued."

"Then she's dead," Elias said.

"I'm not going to lay any bets on that," Mike Donovan told him. "Goddamn it, when are we going to get power? We don't know *what* she was saying, or to whom. We've got to get to her."

"I agree," Julie said. She crossed the command center to Martin. "Do we have power yet?" she asked.

Martin looked at her a moment, then moved to another console. He flipped switches and examined the telltales which lit up.

"Not yet," he told her. "Both the engines that went down are completely out of the circuit, so I'd guess they're still working on them. No, wait . . ." One light changed from orange to blue, and another bank that had been dark came on yellow. "Engine four is back on line," he said. "And it seems to be operational." One by one the yellow lights turned blue. Then another bank of telltales lit up. "Yes," he said. "We've got power on all systems now." He stood away from his console, relief plain on his face. "We can go back to Earth now," he said.

"Not just yet," Elias said, crossing over to him. He looked to Mike and Julie for confirmation. "First we get Diana, right?" His two friends nodded.

"All right," Martin said. "Barbara, you have the coordinates?"

"I'm feeding them in now," Barbara told him.

"Good. We'll be within a mile of her last position in twenty minutes."

Chapter 3

The plant where human beings had been put into suspended animation before being stowed aboard the Mother Ship seemed deserted. No lights shone in the darkness, there was no sound of machinery. The gates in the fence that surrounded the place were closed but unlocked. The damage the rebels had caused in their abortive raid some months back had been repaired, and there were no signs of subsequent fighting. Isolated as it was from the rest of the community, it had not suffered vigilante wrath following the departure of the Mother Ships.

Still, Ham Tyler, Robert Maxwell, Chris Faber, and the other rebels who had come in five trucks were cautious. The weather had prevented the toxin from drifting to this area, and while most of the Visitors had been recalled to their ships, it was entirely possible that there would be a few survivors.

"You go take a look around that side," Ham told Fred Linker, a middle-aged man who had been a lawyer before the Visitors' arrival. "This place is just too neat. If it was abandoned all of a sudden, there should be some disorder, but there isn't."

Fred nodded and, tapping a woman named Claire Bryant and another man named Paul Overbloom to join him, started working his way around to the right, keeping well back from the fence. When they were out of sight, the Fixer turned to another rebel, a woman named Grace Delaney, whose husband had disappeared into the plant some months before.

"I want you to spread the others out to right and left here while Chris and Maxwell and I go in," he told her.

"Let me come in with you," she demanded.

"No, Grace, you're too personally involved. If there are Visitors in there, I want them alive. But if you hear shots, then it will be up to you to get us out, okay?"

"I don't like it, Ham," she said. "We shouldn't keep prisoners even if there are survivors."

"Then who are we going to use to deprocess people when Mike comes back?" Robert Maxwell asked her.

"The equipment can't be that complicated," Grace said. "I'll bet Barry Stine and I could figure it out, if you give us a chance."

"You may have to," Ham Tyler told her, "but we'll do it my way first. I want you at my back, because I know you'll do whatever needs to be done if we need help, okay?"

"All right, Ham, but if you don't come out in ten minutes, I'm coming in whether I hear shots or not."

"Fair enough," Tyler said. Then with Robert Maxwell on his right and Chris Faber on his left, he walked boldly toward the fence and the gate.

They had just stepped through when the sound of a Visitor weapon going off came from the far side of the building, followed almost immediately by a brief return volley.

"Keep this side covered," Ham called to Grace, then he and Robert and Chris ran around the building. There were no other shots. They came to the front where the offices were located and found Fred Linker and his companions kneeling over a figure in a red uniform that was lying half out of the front doorway.

"It's a Visitor," Fred said, looking up. "He's not wearing any armor, and his shot was so wild he can't have been a soldier, but look at this." He rolled the body over onto its back. Covering the dead Visitor's mouth and nose was a close-fitting, circular respirator.

They stepped over the body and entered the darkened building. The reception area was empty, but a door on the far side led to other offices and eventually back into the plant proper. Ham, his gun drawn, eased himself into the corridor.

"Don't shoot," an oddly muffled but distinctly alien female voice called from a partly open door at the far end.

"Throw out your guns," Ham Tyler barked.

"We don't have any," the voice answered. "Louie had the only one."

"All right," Ham said while Chris found a switch and flooded the place with light. "Come on out with your hands up."

The door opened slowly and the speaker, also wearing a respirator, emerged, her hands high over her head. Claire and Paul quickly went up to her and checked her for weapons while Fred looked into the room from which the Visitor had emerged.

"Three dead in here," he called back.

"How many more are you?" Robert asked the Visitor.

"Only twelve alive—eleven now, including me," she answered. "That's all the respirators there were."

"All right," Ham said. "Fred, you get back to Grace and make sure she doesn't start shooting just for the fun of it." Fred nodded and went back out the front door.

Ham Tyler and the others quickly looked into the other offices on the floor. In each room they found three or four dead Visitors. By the time they finished, they could hear Grace Delaney and the others moving through the larger plant area in back.

"There should be ten more of you," Ham said to their prisoner. "Where are they?"

"Upstairs, in the executive suite," the Visitor woman answered.

"Show us the way," Robert Maxwell said. The prisoner, her hands now clasped behind her head, nodded toward an el at the other end of the corridor. Taking her with them, they turned the corner to see Grace and several other rebels coming from the far end where the corridor entered the main processing area.

"Nobody back here," Grace said, "at least not alive."

"I thought the toxin hadn't spread this far," Claire Bryant said as the two groups joined. Grace Delaney looked at the prisoner with an obvious urge to kill.

"Toy balloons," the prisoner said. "They floated down all

around the place this afternoon. We didn't know what they meant, but when Nancy shot one just for fun, this red dust came out of it, and she went into convulsions. That's when those of us who could got the respirators."

"What did you need respirators in this plant for," Grace asked suspiciously.

"The heat exchangers use a toxic cooling fluid. We keep respirators just in case we have to make repairs."

"All right," Tyler said. "Now let's go find the rest of your friends. Where are the stairs?"

"Through that door there," the Visitor told him.

"Claire," Ham said, "Paul, you stay here with our guest. The rest of you, come with me. Keep alert, but don't shoot unless you have to. I mean it, Grace."

The woman rebel glared at him, but holstered her pistol.

The stairs, broad and curving up a circular well, led them to a corridor identical to the one below. The branch of the el going toward the back opened onto a large, glass-enclosed observation balcony. Two bodies lay huddled at the far end.

Several doors opened off the main corridor which crossed the front of the building. The rooms beyond the first three were a bathroom, a kitchen, and a small dining room. In the last were three Visitors, sitting slumped over the octagonal table. Chris Faber checked each one. "Just making sure nobody's playing possum," he explained.

As they neared the far end of the corridor, they could see that the inner wall was of glass, with a glass door at either end. The room on the other side of the glass was dark, illumined only by the light that came through from the corridor. Ham and Robert, their guns drawn, slid down the wall across from the window until they could see inside.

It was a large conference room with an oval table and chairs drawn up all around it. The surviving Visitors, all wearing respirators, were sitting there watching the glass. As soon as they saw Tyler and Maxwell, they all raised their arms in surrender.

"We got them," the Fixer told the others as he holstered his pistol. He went to the door and stepped inside, Robert and Chris at his heels.

"Isn't this a pretty sight," Ham said. The Visitors slowly got to their feet.

"Please don't shoot," one of them said, his resonant voice muffled by the device over his mouth and nose. "We're not armed."

"Turn around and put your hands against the wall," Ham ordered. As the Visitors complied, several rebels holstered their weapons and went around the table to search the prisoners.

"Why didn't you go back to the Mother Ship?" Robert Maxwell asked.

"We didn't have a chance," one of the Visitors, a woman, told him. "The last shuttle of suspendees left just before the soldiers were ordered to return to the ship. We waited for one to come for us, but it never did."

"So you were abandoned," Ham said. "Maybe you were lucky."

"Do any of you know how to operate this plant?" Robert asked as the rebels concluded their search.

"Yes," the woman said, turning around to face him. "Most of us were technicians. I'm a supervisor. There were only twenty soldiers here."

"All right," Ham said. "We think our people have captured your Mother Ship. If they have, they'll be bringing it here to unload the people you put into suspended animation. Can you reverse the process?"

"We can."

"That's fine, and as long as you cooperate, you won't get hurt. Now let's go downstairs. But I warn you, some of us here have relatives aboard that ship and might be a little inclined to take vengeance if you make the slightest wrong move. Get me?"

The Visitors nodded. Then, under the supervision of the rebels, they all filed out of the conference room and down the main floor of the plant.

There Grace Delaney came up to Tyler, her face angry.

"There are about a hundred people here," she said, "humans—in those damned plastic coffins." She glared at the prisoners. "What are we going to do about it?"

"Put these Visitors to work," Ham said. "That's why we wanted them alive."

"I still say Barry and I can figure out how to work the equipment."

"Let's go take a look," Robert said. Grace called Barry Stine, a stocky young black man, and they went past conveyors and tables to a hulking machine the size of a station wagon projecting from a side wall. From one end a conveyor projected, leading across the floor to a loading dock at the back.

Grace and Barry, with Robert watching, lifted up the covers concealing the control panel. "It should be all automatic," Grace said, "once it's set up and started." She stared at the dials and knobs. Each one bore a legend, a small label printed in the alien's alphabet.

"I can't read this stuff," Barry complained.

"That's the master switch, I think," Grace said, pointing to a heavy, black lever. Barry moved around to the side, took out a Swiss army knife, opened a screwdriver blade, and began unfastening an inner cover. When he got it off he looked inside at the wires, tubing, and gears that surrounded the device's inner chamber.

"I don't think so," he said. "It looks more like a coolant dump."

"Damn!" Grace swore. "Are you sure?"

"No, it might be a recycling filter."

"Why take a chance, Grace?" Maxwell asked gently.

"We can figure out their electronics," Grace complained, "so why not this?"

"Because in many ways their electronics is similar to ours. But this is nothing like a meat-packing plant."

"But that's just what it *is*."

"I know it is, in effect, but can you see *any* similarity between the Hormel plant where you worked and this machinery?"

"None at all," Barry Stine said. "I sure would hate to use up a couple dozen people trying to figure this out. Hell, Grace; we could destroy this equipment before we ever learned how to make it work."

"Let the technicians do their job," Robert said. "Every

human revival is a test, and they know that if they fail even once, if even one human doesn't make it, they'll be killed. We've got to trust them that far."

"All right," Grace Delaney said, "but I'm going to keep a damn close eye on them."

"You do that," Robert told her.

It was not yet morning, but the suspension plant was in operation. One by one, under the watchful eyes of the rebels, the humans who had been placed in plastic coffins were being brought back to consciousness. With only a fraction of the usual staff, it was a slow process. After two hours, only ten of the one hundred people intended for the Visitors' larder had been revived. They were disoriented at first, weak and groggy, but after twenty minutes or so they were able to sit up, talk coherently if slowly, and even walk around a little.

"This is impossible," Robert Maxwell said angrily. He and Ham Tyler were sitting in the cab of one of the trucks, all of which had been brought into the loading area at the back of the plant. "We're going to have to deal with ten *thousand* people. It could take forever to reprocess all of them."

"It doesn't hurt people to stay in those cans, does it?" the Fixer asked. He had his seat pushed back as far as it would go so he could stretch out his legs. Fully half the rebels were similarly disposed, or in the backs of the trucks trying to catch up on their sleep.

"I don't know," Maxwell said, "but it can't do them much good. On the ship each of those plastic coffins is hooked up to a life-support system. Without that, people could die before they get revived."

"What we're going to have to do," Fred Linker said, coming to the window on Robert's side of the truck, "is have these technicians teach some of us how to operate the equipment, so we can have all ten lines going full speed instead of just one at quarter speed."

"I think Grace and Barry are already working on that," Robert said, "but how long will that training take?"

"It may not make any difference," Ham said, stifling a

yawn, "if Donovan doesn't bring the ship back. *That's* what I'm worried about."

Paul Overbloom, who'd been standing watch by the loading dock, came rushing over to them.

"We've got company," he said. "Lots of cops, and I don't like the way they're distributing themselves around the plant."

"Probably think there's nobody but Visitors in here," Ham said, getting out of the truck. Robert followed suit. "Where's Chris?" Tyler asked.

"I'll get him," Paul said, and went off to find Ham's colleague.

"I guess," Ham said, buckling on his holster, "we'd better go out there and let them know the score. No sense being raided by our own people."

Robert walked with him over to the loading dock, where they were met by Paul and Chris Faber. Chris pulled open one half of the sliding double door and the four of them stepped out onto the dock. The sky was still dark, but the plant's paved yard was lit by overhead lights. Their company, who were all inside the fence and arranged along its length, consisted of half a dozen motorcycle cops and three state-police cars, beside each of which stood four officers.

The police became fully alert as the four rebels came out onto the dock. One of the officers by a car, a captain who seemed to be in charge, cast wary glances at his men, then stepped forward to speak to the rebels.

"Take off your guns, please," he said, "and come down over here."

"You might explain what's going on first," Tyler said, making no move to disarm himself.

"You're trespassing on private property," the officer said, "and you're all under arrest." The other officers casually placed their hands on their sidearms.

"Look, Captain, maybe you don't understand. This is the installation the Visitors were using to kidnap people and send them up to their ship in cans."

"I wouldn't know about that," the captain said, "but I've got my orders. Now, are you going to come quietly, or is it going to have to be unpleasant?"

"It's damn well unpleasant already," Robert Maxwell said

angrily. "We've got one hundred citizens in here in a state of suspended animation, and we're trying to revive them."

"You and who else?" the captain asked, trying to conceal his surprise.

"Twenty of us and eleven Visitors," Ham Tyler said. "Now, are you going to let us go on about our business, or would you rather a lot of innocent people suffered because of your interference?"

The captain backed away, and the other police, digesting this bit of news, began to move to places of concealment.

"Let's get back inside," Chris muttered. Paul backed up to the door, Chris following him. Ham just turned around as if he weren't concerned, and Robert, anticipating a shot, sidled to the door while keeping his hand on his own gun. He pulled the sliding door shut just as one of the motorcycle cops took aim and fired.

"What the hell's going on out there?" Grace Delaney called from her place by the processing machine. All work had stopped at the sound of the shot, and every rebel was on his or her feet, guns drawn.

"We're being arrested for trespassing," Ham said sardonically. He and Chris went to a window from which they could scan the paved yard. They were joined by several others, who began to prepare to defend the place.

"Now hold it," Robert said, "if they start shooting, some of those shots could hit innocent people in here."

"So what do we do," Tyler demanded, "just give up? Dammit, I haven't fought the Visitors this long only to be hauled in by a bunch of local cops."

"So fight them somewhere else," Maxwell demanded. "If these machines are damaged by gunfire, we may never revive all those people on the ship."

"All right," Ham said, backing away from the window and reholstering his gun. "That's a good point." He turned to Chris. "Get everybody in the trucks. We're going to break out."

"Visitors too?" Chris asked.

"Yes," Robert said. "We'll need them later, when this is straightened out."

"How about the people we've revived?"

"We're going to leave them to the tender mercies of the highway patrol," Ham said. Chris went off to get everybody organized. "We don't have room for them," Ham explained to Robert, "and the ones still in cans will be better off here."

"But those people are helpless," Robert protested.

"The cops will see that," Ham said, and turned to Fred Linker who was climbing into the driver's seat of one of the five trucks. "You take the Visitors back to the lighthouse," he said. "The rest of us will have to find a new base. We'll let you know where it is as soon as we can."

"Okay," Fred said. "I think Grace and Barry ought to come along too. They're the only ones who have any idea how this stuff works."

"Good idea," Ham said. He grabbed Paul Overbloom as he came by. "Go to a window and talk to those people out there," he told him. "Just keep them occupied so they don't come charging in shooting." Paul nodded, then the Fixer started directing people to the various vehicles.

When everybody was sorted out to Ham's satisfaction, he came back to Fred's truck. "You first," he said. "They'll be surprised, and you should be able to get clear before they start shooting." Fred nodded and started his engine.

"All right, Chris," he called to his colleague, who was standing by Paul, who was still stalling the cops. "Robert and I will be in the last truck. When Fred is clear, start shooting. Just make those cops keep their heads down. Then you pile in when we go by."

"Gotcha," Chris said. Two other rebels went to the main doors, and on Fred's signal, pulled them aside. Overbloom accelerated as hard as he could, leaving rubber on the plant floor. The police were indeed taken by surprise and had to jump out of Fred's way as he roared toward the gate, knocking over two motorcycles as he passed through. Then Chris, Paul, and the two rebels at the door started shooting.

The second truck followed seconds after the first, then the third and the fourth. The police, now disorganized and forced to take cover by the shooting from inside the plant, fired several times at the trucks as they sped past, but return fire from the rebels riding in the vehicles kept them from being effective. Then Tyler gunned his engine, drove toward the door, hesitated just a second as the last four rebels climbed in back, then came out at full speed. Several police bullets hit the side of the truck as they passed through the gate, but none of the rebels were hit.

A half hour later, having thrown off pursuit, the convoy of trucks pulled over at the highway interchange where they would split up. The sun was just coming up, shining red fire off the windshields of several cars that had been abandoned by the side of the road. Ham and Robert had decided on a new base, and Robert Maxwell got out to tell Fred Linker where they would be.

"The San Pedro Municipal Building is right in the middle of town," he said. "When you get back to the lighthouse, see if you can't have Linda and Alice rig us a communicator for you to bring down, so we can keep in touch."

"I'll do that," Fred said. Then he started his engine again and rolled off up the on ramp.

Ham Tyler and Chris Faber were standing beside the truck when Robert got back. "I'll see you at the base a little later," Ham said.

"Where are you going?"

"I want to get hold of the network, to see if I can find out who gave orders to have us arrested," Ham explained. "Calling us trespassers was just an excuse." He went over to one of the abandoned cars and looked in the driver's seat. "Think you can get this started?" he asked Chris.

"Unless it's out of gas," the large man said.

"Be careful," Robert told Ham as Chris popped the hood and started to fiddle inside.

"You too," Ham said, shaking his hand.

Then Robert got in behind the wheel of his truck, and the caravan started moving again.

Chapter 4

The three-mile-diameter disk of the alien Mother Ship
that had once floated over Los Angeles now hung in space
between the Earth and the moon, which, from this position,
seemed of equal size. Perhaps a mile off, a mere sand-grain by
comparison, was Diana's escape shuttle. Though both craft
seemed to be motionless in relation to each other, they were in
fact speeding toward the moon, which imperceptibly grew
larger as the moments passed.

From the hollowed-out underbody of the Mother Ship, two
more shuttles dropped into the blackness of space. The central
modules of these two craft were different from those in which
passengers or cargo were carried. Less bulky, each sported a
thick, sturdy fin on either side, the fins ending in nearly
spherical knobs a yard in diameter.

The two tug shuttles approached Diana's craft, one on either
side, slowing cautiously as they came within firing range. The
escape shuttle did not respond to them but just hung there, its
ports dark. The tugs drifted closer now, aligning themselves
beside the escape shuttle, pointing in the same direction. Then
once more they moved, slipping sideways until the knobs
nearest the escape shuttle nearly touched it. There was a
sudden crackling spark, silent in the airlessness as the
magnetic clamps took hold of Diana's craft. Still there was no
response from the dark shuttle.

As a unit, the three vehicles, held together by powerful magnetic forces, turned and headed back toward the Mother Ship. Their movement was slightly clumsy, with a tendency to yaw, but they made it to the docking bay and floated in.

Inside, the three shuttles settled down to the deck. The two escort tugs then disengaged with more sparks, now loud in the atmosphere of the bay. The tugs lifted up a foot, slid to the side, and settled down again.

Standing well clear of the three shuttles, Mike Donovan, Juliet Parrish, and Maggie Blodgett drew their sidearms. As they approached Diana's craft, the pilots of the two tugs, the fifth columnists Aaron and Peter, disembarked from their craft and joined them.

"She's been without power for a long time," Peter said as they met at the escape craft's port.

"Do you think she's dead?" Julie asked as Aaron touched the port's external lock.

"There's a good chance," Peter said, "but from suffocation rather than cold."

The port didn't open. "There's not enough power left even for that," Aaron said. The two fifth columnists had to manually force the port open before they could go inside.

The air in the escape craft smelled bad, depleted, and they had to wait a moment until the air from the docking bay had had a chance to replace that in the shuttle. Then with Mike and Julie in the lead, the five went forward into the cockpit.

Though her command chair was turned away from them, facing the shuttle's main ports, they could see Diana's arms, hanging limply from either side. Mike went cautiously up to her and spoke.

"Diana?" There was no response. He reached out and touched her shoulder. "God, she's frozen," he exclaimed. With Julie to help, he undid her seat belt and pulled her out of the command chair. Maggie and Peter took hold of her upper torso while Mike and Julie took her legs. She was very cold, and stiff. They laid her down near the hatch where Aaron could take a look at her.

"She's still alive," he said after touching her throat and abdomen, "but just barely. We'd better get her to the infirmary right away."

Mike leaned out of the hatch. "Got that stretcher?" he called.

"Right here," William answered from outside. He wheeled the medical cart up to the hatch and held it in place while the others moved Diana onto it. Then Julie jumped down from the shuttle and took an antitoxin pill from a pocket. Peter forced Diana's mouth open while Juliet dropped in the pill, then massaged the unconscious woman's throat until she swallowed involuntarily.

"Can't have her dying on us now," Maggie Blodgett said grimly.

"That would hardly be satisfactory," Donovan agreed. "In the first place, she's going to stand trial. But more important, she knows things we need to know."

"Such as how to deconvert people," Julie said.

"The only question is," Maggie asked, "will she tell us anything?"

Off to one side of the docking bay, partially concealed by other shuttles, three Visitor trustees stood watching. As had been done with other trustees, the sleeves had been torn off their uniforms just above their elbows to distinguish them from known fifth columnists. They stepped back farther out of sight as Diana's stretcher was wheeled away.

"I think she's alive," Richard said. "What do you think they're going to do with her?"

"I don't know," Gretchen answered, "but I think I can find out."

"If they catch you spying," Valery cautioned, "they'll lock you up with the others."

"I'll be careful. But she's our commander, after all."

"You're not thinking of trying to rescue her?" Richard asked.

Gretchen gave him a hard glance. "At least not until we're closer to Earth and have a chance of getting away."

"But she wanted to destroy Earth," Richard protested. "She's a criminal, and probably insane."

"That's as may be. I know where my loyalty lies." She turned to Valery. "How about you?"

"I'm not very fond of Diana," Valery said slowly, "but she is, after all, one of our race."

"Earth humans are people too," Richard said, "even if they are mammals."

"Even?" Valery snapped. "We're not talking about scale patterns, Richard, we're talking about a very fundamental difference. No, I don't think I owe these *relavish* any allegiance."

"In spite of what you told Peter and Martin?"

"In spite of that," Valery said. She and Gretchen looked at him meaningfully.

The infirmary room was a special one that they'd set up just for this occasion. The doors could not be opened from the inside, and there were restraints on the bed. The cabinets were all securely locked, and the ventilation hatches were welded in place.

The door opened and William entered, towing Diana's stretcher, with Aaron pushing from behind. Mike Donovan and Juliet Parrish followed soon after. The four lifted Diana from the stretcher, placed here on the bed, and fastened straps across her arms and legs. Then Aaron took a key and unlocked a closet. Inside was a monitoring device on a small wheeled table. He rolled this over to the bed and started attaching probes to Diana's head, throat, chest, and abdomen.

Aaron explained the purpose of each connection as he made it, in terms that Julie understood but that Donovan and William found totally incomprehensible. Julie was fascinated by the procedure, but when she asked Aaron how the monitoring machine worked, he was unable to answer.

"I'm only a medical assistant," he said. "It would take a doctor and an electronics expert to explain this machine to you. I'm sorry."

"But you know how to read the device?" Mike asked.

"In large part. I couldn't identify most of the less common diseases, but I should be able to tell you if Diana's all right or not."

He switched on the machine. Needles on an array of dials moved, some of them into the green zone at the left. "Those are danger areas," he explained. "Our dials read the opposite of yours."

There was also a bank of lights, some yellow, some blue, some orange. A few lights were unlit. "Those are for tests we're not doing," Aaron went on. "The blue means stable, the orange means there's a problem, and the yellow means marginal." He flipped more switches and watched as the lights changed colors and the needles changed position.

"It's just like I figured," he went on. "Simple anoxia complicated by mild supercooling." He flipped switches again. "She's already recovering and should regain consciousness in a few minutes."

"Is there anything we should do?" Julie asked. "Administer oxygen, heat?"

"I don't think it will be necessary," Aaron told her. "Besides, I'm not quite sure of the procedure."

The door opened and Caleb Taylor came in. "I think we've got trouble," he said. "One of the trustees, I think his name was Richard, was found murdered down in the docking bay a few minutes ago."

"What happened?" Juliet asked. "Do you know who did it?"

"He was strangled," Caleb said, "and his neck was broken. As for who, nobody's saying, of course, though I think some of them might know the truth. Other than the murderers, I mean."

Mike Donovan turned to Willaim. "Did you know this guy Richard?" he asked.

"Not very well," William said. "He was just a worker like me. I do remember once he said he didn't like having been lied to about humans being the same as cattle."

"It sounds," Aaron said, "as if he overheard some kind of plot and got silenced."

"What kind of plot could there be?" Julie asked.

"A sixth column," Caleb said. "Visitors who don't want to go along with Martin and Barbara."

"I'm afraid that's possible," Aaron said. "Diana was not well liked, but she could inspire fanatical loyalty and devotion among some of us."

"Do you suppose any of the fifth columnists would be in on this plot?" Mike asked.

"None that joined before the final battle," Aaron said, "but among the trustees, yes."

"I don't think we can trust any of them," Caleb said, "even those who have reported on others trying to stop work. And get this: some of these so-called trustees have been heard to say that they think our two races should be kept separate." He laughed harshly. "Can you believe that?"

"There's more differences between them and us," Mike said to the black man, "than between you and me."

"Oh, I know that. I'm just not used to being considered part of the upper class holding the minority race in subjugation." He laughed again. "No offense, Willie," he added.

"I think I'd better go talk with Martin," Donovan said. "This business is going to have to be stopped before it gets out of hand."

"I'll go with you," Caleb said, and the two left.

"I hate to say this," Aaron said as the door closed behind them, "but I think bringing Diana on board is what's started the trouble."

"I believe you're right," Julie said. "We should have been more secretive about it." She went to stand by the head of Diana's bed. "I think she's beginning to come around."

Aaron checked the monitor again and agreed. Even as he disconnected the wires and probes, Diana's breathing began to change.

"Don't say anything about this counterrebellion," Julie whispered. "We need all the advantage we can get."

Diana moaned and then became very still for a moment. Her breathing deepened, and then her eyes opened. She was fully awake. She tried to move one arm just once, but stopped as soon as she felt the restraints. Her expression was calm and grim, but a slight smile turned up the corners of her mouth.

"You seem to have won," she said.

"We have," Julie answered. "We're in control of your ship, and we're on our way back to Earth right now."

"Yet you went to the effort of rescuing me," Diana said. "You could have just let me drift. Why didn't you?"

"That would have been the easy way out, wouldn't it?"

Julie said. "We rescued you for two reasons. First, you're going to stand trial for what your people did to us and to our planet."

"Hah!" Diana barked. "How fair a trial do you suppose that will be?"

"Probably not fair at all, but that doesn't really matter. It's the symbolism that counts. You represent the evil that was done to us, and your trial will symbolize our victory over that evil. But more than that, you owe us compensation. You were the science officer of your fleet, Diana, and what you know will help us recover from the damage you have done, and may even give us an advantage."

"You don't think I'm going to *cooperate* with you, do you?" Diana sneered.

"If we can figure out how to work the conversion machine," Julie said coldly, "you may not have a choice."

"Never," Diana said. "It takes years of training, a staff of experts, and a fine artistic touch to perform a conversion."

"Well, at the least, we'll have you to experiment on. And if we damage you in the process, what more fitting punishment could there be for your crimes?"

The defiance slowly faded from Diana's face.

"Now, remember," Valery told the three trustees, "be very careful who you talk to."

"That's right," Gretchen said. "If in doubt, don't mention our plan at all. We can't just kill everybody who won't go along with us."

"For one thing," Valery said, "we could find ourselves killing so many we couldn't operate the ship."

"And for another," Gretchen said, "if too many die, those *relavish* will start cracking down on us and cramp our style."

"Once there are enough of us we can take over the command center," Valery said, "a lot of others will follow along."

"And even if they don't," Gretchen said as the three new recruits nodded their understanding, "there are plenty of people in security who will support us once we can set them free."

"But what are we going to do about weapons?" one of the

three trustees, an older man named Luke, asked. "They're in contaminated areas."

"We'll have to get respirators," Valery said. "But we'll worry about that later. Right now just slow down. Pretend to cooperate but drag your heels. And check out everybody you know."

"But carefully," Gretchen said. "Very carefully."

Chapter 5

San Pedro, once a town of 35,000, stood empty. The only inhabitants were birds, squirrels, insects, a few starving dogs and cats—and fifteen rebels, who occupied the top floor of the municipal building with their trucks concealed among the abandoned vehicles in the parking basement below.

Robert Maxwell, senior among them, was their de facto leader. He was not used to this kind of role. He had proved his worth as Juliet Parrish's lieutenant and Ham Tyler's captain, but he had no experience leading people on his own initiative. Worrying about his children and the other rebels who were still at the lighthouse, and about Mike Donovan and Julie and the others aboard the Mother Ship, didn't help any.

He stood now, in what had once been some minor official's office, looking out over the abandoned city. Cars, some just parked, others overturned or blown up, were scattered along the street. In places the pavement had been torn up. Stores stood with their windows broken, their doors open. He and the other rebels had plenty of food, though there was no power and they had to depend on bottled water.

He heard the door open behind him and turned to see Claire Bryant come in with a plate of canned food and a bottle of warm cola.

"We missed you at supper," Claire said. Robert turned back to the window. The sun was going down, and soon the sky would be full of color. "You should eat something," Claire persisted.

"I know," Maxwell said. "Just put it on the desk."

"You did the right thing," Claire told him. She put the plate down amid the clutter of paperwork that now would never be finished, and came over to stand beside him. "Keep the fighting force together and mobile, and save the lighthouse for the others. We would have endangered the children if we'd gone back there."

"Yes," he said, "that was my motive." He looked at her profile. Since Kathleen's death, he hadn't really paid much attention to women, but Claire Bryant was something special. Not the same as his wife, but as strong as Kathleen had been. He put the thought out of his mind. It was too soon to become involved yet.

"There's another child I'm worried about," he went on.

"Elizabeth?"

"Yes, her too, but I meant Sean."

"Mike's boy. Yes."

"He wasn't at the Visitor Headquarters. His grandmother must have sent him somewhere else."

"Or his stepgrandfather, Arthur, took him? He wasn't there either."

"I know. I hope Sean's all right. If we don't find the boy, or at least discover where he is, Mike will be frantic when he gets back."

"Sean's mother is up on that ship, isn't she?" Claire asked rhetorically.

"Yes, along with most of the people of San Pedro. I don't know how many of them are still alive. The ship holds ten thousand, but there were more than three times that many here before the Visitors took them away."

"And the rest? Eaten?"

"Or on other ships, and now beyond our reach. Fifty ships, Claire! Fifty times ten thousand or more. That's at least half a million people. And there's nothing we can do about them."

"Well, most of them, but we'll get some of them back when Mike and Julie return."

"It's been so long," Robert said. "I'm beginning to lose hope."

"I'm afraid a lot of the rest of us are too," Claire admitted.

Robert's stomach growled. In spite of his anxiety and concern, he was hungry. It had been a long time since he'd eaten. He went to sit at the desk and pulled the plastic plate of corned-beef hash and cold canned beans toward him. "You forgot the fork," he said.

"I'm sorry," Claire said. She pulled one from her shirt pocket and handed it to him.

"Thanks." He started to eat. "Any word from Ham?"

"No, but I forgot to tell you, we got the communicator from the lighthouse. Fred Linker brought it in just a few minutes ago."

Someone had rigged up a small gasoline-powered generator in a windowed closet, and from there had run wires into the large conference room. There they'd set up a television high on the wall where everybody could watch it. Other wires led to the communicator, which was set up in the antechamber, where someone was always listening.

Six or seven of the rebels, including Paul Overbloom and Fred Linker, sat watching the screen. It felt strange to watch regular programming, situation comedies, and dramas. For the rebels, the world was a different place, and it took an effort to remember that for 95 percent of the population, the whole episode of the Visitors had merely been a bad dream of confusion, high prices, limited communications, and shortages. The country still went on, though the artificial stability that had been imposed by the Visitors was missing, and the shakiness of the remaining government was becoming obvious.

The one real difference now was that five-minute news bulletins came on every hour instead of just at six and eleven, with occasional special bulletins on the half hour. The faces of familiar news anchormen and women kept reporting progress in reestablishing order, but as likely as not, the reports were contradicted by the next bulletins announcing outbreaks of revelry or looting.

Radical groups both new and old, sensitive to the ever more obvious power vacuum, staged demonstrations, marches, and conferences, demanding that governmental and economic recovery include their ideas for the formation of a perfect state.

Other news stories told about rebel groups similar to theirs. Some had returned home with little or no difficulty, accepted by their communities as heroes, or at least as well-intentioned malcontents. Others were having more trouble, and were accused of treason, trespass, or collaboration. Still others, having found the rebel life preferable to what they'd experienced before, had chosen to remain rebels against their own people, seeking to wrest power by force of arms.

"That kind of helps explain the reception we got at the suspension plant," Fred Linker said.

"I'm not sure, I believe all those stories," Paul demurred. "God knows we're heroes, but if we'd been captured by those cops at the plant, we'd be counted among the bad guys."

"Hey," somebody said, "that's *us* they're talking about!" The room got very quiet.

". . . in Pomona," the announcer was saying, "a group of Visitor sympathizers had taken over the building where, reportedly, human victims had been put into suspended animation prior to being taken up to the Mother Ship. Police Captain Emil Jonkers said that attempts had been made to 'process' more human victims. Approximately eighty-five people were found in a comatose condition, and another fifteen were returned to their homes in a state of confusion. The sympathizers managed to escape by running down state police and highway patrol officers in their trucks. Police vehicles were damaged in the gunfight preceding the escape, so pursuit was not possible, according to Jonkers."

"Those bastards have got it all wrong," Paul Overbloom yelled, and he was not alone in his protest.

"How can they believe that stuff?" Fred asked angrily.

"Hell, people will believe anything on the news."

"No, I mean the police. They must have talked to those people we revived. 'State of confusion,' my ass. The *police* are the sympathizers, not us. Somebody fed them a line."

"I guess that's what the Fixer went to find out about," Paul said. The two men, still fuming, turned their attention back to the TV.

The screen showed grim shots of Visitors, stripped of their

human disguises, hanging from lamp posts. The reporter told of others, who had somehow survived the toxin, being kept in local jails. "Apparently," the announcer said, "one in every five hundred aliens has a natural immunity to the toxin released yesterday by liberation forces."

"That's not the best news I've heard," Fred said. The bulletin ended, to be replaced by an episode of *Dr. Who*.

Robert Maxwell and Claire Bryant came in just as Tom Baker was outwitting some kind of slime monster with the help of a scantily clad huntress.

"You should have seen the latest bulletin," Fred Linker said, and told them about the report of their escape from the suspension plant. As he listened, Robert felt the weight of responsibility drag his shoulders down until he had to take a chair. Claire put a comforting hand on his shoulder.

"That captain told us he had his orders," Maxwell said. "All I can figure is that whoever gave those orders is somebody the Visitors converted."

"That makes sense," Paul Overbloom said. "The whole reason for the conversion process was to make government officials sympathetic to the Visitors."

"But the Visitors are gone now," Claire protested.

"Yes, but don't you see?" Fred said. "With the Visitors gone, the converted people are like cars without drivers. They're still moving the way the Visitors wanted them to, but now they're out of control."

"And they still tend to see things the Visitors' way," Robert Maxwell agreed. "The President, for one, and the most influential members of Congress."

"Right," Paul said, "and governors and mayors of large cities like Los Angeles."

"He hasn't been seen in weeks," Claire Bryant said.

"Well, New York, then, or Chicago. Who knows how many generals and admirals are out there converted but no longer controlled?"

"We can't trust our own leaders anymore," Fred said.

"Or our best scientists," Robert added. "They were the first to go. Remember Corley Walker?"

"This is terrible," Claire said. "I thought we'd won. But the people we need most—our government, the psychologists, anthropologists, doctors—they were the Visitors' prime targets for conversion. We might as well have been blown up."

"Quiet back there," somebody called. "There's a special bulletin on."

It was Dennis W. Simon, the Lieutenant Governor, speaking from the governor's mansion in Sacramento.

"As of six o'clock this afternoon," he said, speaking into a bank of microphones, "I have assumed the responsibility of acting Governor in the absence of Abe Riggsbee who, with certain members of his staff, disappeared from the mansion four weeks ago. Every effort is being made to locate Governor Riggsbee, but we must be prepared to accept the possibility that he, along with so many others, has fallen victim to an as yet unidentified scheme perpetrated by the Visitors."

"Does he really not know?" Paul asked.

"The Visitors have left us now," Simon was saying, "but the crisis is not yet past. Indeed, we are only now beginning to become aware of the extent of the damage done us. It is for this reason that I have decided that California will remain in a state of martial law for the next two weeks."

"Or as long as it suits him," Fred Linker said.

"During this time," Simon said, "I urge each and every one of you to cooperate with the police, both state and local, to the full extent of your ability, and to cooperate with National Guardsmen, should they require it.

"Our objective is first to determine the full extent of the crisis and, second, to immediately implement measures to restore normal order. This will not be easy, but progress is already being made, and with your cooperation our objective can be more readily reached."

"He's so damned slick," Fred muttered. "Has *he* been converted?"

"In addition," the Lieutenant Governor went on, "we must immediately cease this senseless slaughter of those whose poor judgment caused them to collaborate with the Visitors. Known collaborators will be put under arrest and tried to determine the extent of their crime, if any. It is not up to you, as vigilantes, to judge these people. It is the responsibility of the state and duly constituted judges and juries.

"More importantly, we must make every effort to insure the safety of those few Visitors who are still alive. All such Visitors must immediately be given over to the custody of local or state authorities, who have been instructed as to how to insure their survival. Personal vengeance taken upon these Visitors will be treated the same as murder. Alive, they can teach us much, with or without their active cooperation. Dead, they can teach us nothing."

He stepped back from the microphones, indicating that he had finished, and immediately began taking questions from the reporters assembled before him.

"It's almost worse than before," Fred said to Robert, Paul, and Claire. "Then we knew who our enemies were. Now who can tell? Is Simon being straight with us? Is he taking advantage of the situation to enhance his own power? Is he a convert whose actions are half-random? How can we tell?"

"I can't answer that," Robert Maxwell said, "but we may learn something when Ham gets back. If he can find out who put out the order to arrest us at the plant, we can be sure that that person is still a Visitor puppet."

"I wish to hell Julie would come back," Claire said. "With her leadership, we were a fighting force, without her, we seem to be becoming just refugees."

"I agree," Robert said. "I'm not the one to fill her shoes."

Chapter 6

"Can't you make it go faster?" Mike Donovan asked. He was standing, looking over Martin's shoulder as the fifth column leader sat at the ship's controls. Other positions were occupied by trustees, under the watchful eye of human and fifth column guards.

"I'm sorry, Mike," Martin said. "If I push it too hard, we'll start breaking up. This ship was never meant to move through the Earth's atmosphere as fast as it did when we left. The structural damage is more extensive than I thought."

"How long will it take to repair?"

"Without a major maintenance facility, several months. We just don't have the equipment or the personnel aboard. All we can do is hold the ship together. We'd need orbiting docking frames, megaton clamps, full-scale stress analyzers, and then it would take more than a week."

"I'm afraid of what's been happening back home since we've been gone," Mike said, explaining his impatience.

"What could happen?" Martin asked, looking up at his friend.

"I hate to think. Maybe nothing, maybe after all the ships left, everybody started returning to normal. But with so many government officials, at every level, either missing or converted, I just don't see that. And besides, what will people think when this ship comes back? We won't be welcomed with open arms, of that I'm sure."

Diana sat in her new prison, calm and defiant. This was not a simple cell, but a suite that had been specially prepared for her. A sheet of transparent material, not quite either glass or plastic, had been welded to walls, floor, and ceiling, forming a wall through which her every action could be observed. She had the use of three-quarters of the suite, which had been left fully furnished. The only opening in the crystal wall was just large enough to permit passage of the live animals she needed for food. If her captors wanted to take her out, welders would have to come and cut the wall apart.

The front quarter of the suite, which gave access to the corridor beyond, contained four chairs, a table, and a communicator which let Diana's captors talk to her and to the rest of the ship. Three of those chairs were occupied now, by Juliet Parrish, Elias Taylor, and Barbara. On the table in front of Julie was a notepad on which she had been writing.

"Tell us again about that signal you sent," Juliet said. Her voice sounded tired, as if she had asked the question more than once before.

"It was just a distress call," Diana said. Though she was the prisoner, she seemed to be in control of the interrogation.

"To whom?" Elias wanted to know.

"To anybody who might listen. I had hoped that some of the fleet might still be in range."

"What is the range?" Julie asked. Barbara started to say something, but Julie stopped her. "What is the range?" she repeated.

"Accounting for the inverse square law," Diana said, leaning back in her chair and smiling, "it could be infinite. But for practical purposes, about half the diameter of your solar system."

"Is that right?" Julie asked Barbara.

"More or less. Half the diameter means the full radius, of course. If one of our ships were as far as Pluto, the signal could be detected without difficulty."

"That's a very powerful distress call," Elias said.

"No sense whispering—" Diana smiled at him, "—when you're calling for help."

"Of course not," Julie said. "If you need help, you shout. But if you were calling for help, why did you call in code?"

"I knew you would pick up my signal," Diana said. "I didn't want to give you my location."

"A rather useless precaution, since we could find you by locating the signal itself. Which is what we did. So, since just calling gave away your location, what need was there to use code?"

Diana was silent. She no longer smirked, but she didn't look at all concerned.

"I've had enough of this," Elias Taylor said. "She can outtalk all three of us. Hell, she even outtalked her own Supreme Commander. If we want information out of her, we're going to have to use more direct methods."

"And just what do you have in mind?" Julie asked shortly. She sounded more than a little tired.

"A little physical pressure," Elias said, making a wringing motion with his hands.

"No," Juliet said. "I won't allow that."

"You got any better ideas?"

"I will not be party to that kind of brutality," Julie insisted.

"But dammit, she deserves it. How many people died because of her? How many people are prisoners on those other forty-nine ships, to be used as cannon fodder or to be eaten?"

"That doesn't excuse torture on our part."

"I agree," Barbara said, "for what it's worth. Just because Diana is a criminal is no reason for us to act like criminals too."

"But dammit—"

"That's the whole point of the fifth column," Barbara insisted. "We rejected the criminal commands and intentions of our superiors. We forsook loyalty to our government, and even to our people, for a higher loyalty—to all intelligent life. If we stoop to torture and coercion now, we'll be no better than she is."

"What?" Julie said sharply. "Of course we're better than

she is." She seemed to be confused. Her eyes went back to Diana, who appeared unmoved by the conversation.

"I think you need to get some rest," Elias said to Julie. "Barbara's got a good point, I won't argue with that, but sometimes you have to take drastic steps. Why don't you just let me call my father. He'll help me with her. You don't need to know anything about it."

"No," Julie said again. "Absolutely not."

"And yet," Diana said calmly, "you threatened to try to convert me, knowing full well that you could destroy my mind in the process."

"I've changed my mind," Julie said. "We won't convert you until we know how the process works."

"Julie," Barbara said, "Elias is right. You need to catch up on your sleep. We can come back later when you're thinking more clearly."

Julie sighed and covered her face with her hand. "We could *all* use some rest, I guess." She looked up at Elias. "You're not exactly in top form yourself."

"Okay, okay, but I still think she'd be more cooperative if we broke a few fingers."

"Let's discuss it later," Barbara said, getting to her feet. Elias followed suit. "Are you coming?" Barbara asked Julie.

"In a minute." She looked at Diana again. "I'd like to talk with Diana alone for a while."

"What about?" Elias asked.

"About my conversion," Julie said grimly. "Diana pried into the deepest parts of my mind. I want to talk to her about that, and I'd just as soon you didn't hear what she might reveal about me."

"All right," Elias said reluctantly, "but don't take too long. I'll check back here in half an hour, and if you're still here, I'll drag you away and force a sleeping pill down your throat."

"Just a few minutes," Julie said, "that's all I need."

"If you say so, but I'll check anyway."

"Thanks, Elias," Julie said. She reached out and squeezed his hand. "Now, will you please leave us alone for a while?"

Elias nodded, then he and Barbara left the cell.

*   *   *

"I'm worried about Julie," Elias confided to Barbara as they walked through the ship's corridors. "I've never seen her act like that before."

"How do you mean?"

"Well, threatening to use conversion on Diana, especially when she won't let me apply a little pressure. Diana hurt her badly. She may not want to be brutal when it comes to finding out about the code signal, but that's a rational response on her part. A desire for personal vengeance is something else."

"You don't think she'd actually try to do anything?" Barbara asked. "Besides, she can't even get into Diana's part of the suite."

"She could shoot her through the food slot," Elias said. They stopped and looked at each other for a moment, considering the possibility.

"Nah," Elias said, "she's still a doctor. She won't kill unless she actually has to."

"Maybe we should go back and insist that she come with us now," Barbara suggested.

"Give her a little time," Elias said. "I can understand her not wanting us to hear about the secrets Diana might have uncovered. But dammit, I will check on her, and I'll bring Mike with me just to make sure."

Elias Taylor and Barbara entered the command center. Mike Donovan and Martin were sitting at the main controls, relaxing. Other crew and their guards seemed to be taking it easy.

"How's it going?" Elias asked.

"Just a matter of time now," Martin said. "There's nothing more to do until we enter Earth's atmosphere."

"Where's Julie," Donovan asked.

"Having a little private conversation with Diana," Elias answered.

"You left her alone with that woman?"

"It will be all right," Barbara said. "She wanted to talk about what Diana found in her mind during the conversion attempt. She didn't want us to hear all the nasty details."

"That's got to be a strange kind of relationship," Elias said.

"The one person Julie possibly hates is also the one who knows more about what's inside her than Julie herself does."

"The idea of that gives me the creeps," Mike agreed. "I think I'm a pretty nice guy most of the time, but there are some things I wouldn't want even Julie to know."

Elias said, "I told her if she wasn't back here in half an hour that we'd come and get her."

"That's probably a good idea. Were you able to get anything out of Diana?"

"I'm afraid not," Barbara said. "She's a very strong person. I felt like I was pounding my head against that crystal partition in her cell. But I'm pretty sure the coded signal she sent wasn't a distress call, even though she claims it was. It just doesn't make sense, but I don't know what it could be."

"We've got the whole thing recorded," Martin said. "I've been repeatedly running it through that decoding program you wrote for it, Barbara, but that executive encryption system Diana used is still proof against computer analysis. Sometimes I think we've got something, but when I check it, it just doesn't make any sense."

"She did tell us," Elias said, "that she was hoping part of the fleet was still near enough to receive the signal."

"That's not very likely," Martin said. "They had enough of a head start to have gotten completely out of the solar system by the time Diana started sending."

"Could she have been intending the signal for your leader?" Mike asked.

"I suppose so, but it would take almost nine years for him to receive it. And then he'd have to have a receiver aimed right here. Of course, he probably does, but nine years is an awfully long time for a distress signal."

"I think we can forget the idea that it was a distress call," Mike said. "I think she learned something about us, some weakness we don't know about, and wanted that information to get back home, no matter how long it took."

"I suspect you're right," Barbara said. "So that makes it more important than ever that we find out the contents of the message."

* * *

Juliet Parrish sat slouched in her chair in front of the crystal partition. Her eyes were closed, as if in deep exhaustion, but her fingers tapped the blank notepad rhythmically.

"I'd like to know more about this conversion process," she said. Diana, watching from the other side of the crystal wall, said nothing.

"Obviously," Julie went on, "I have a personal interest. I'm still not completely sure about myself. If we could get the cooperation of those conversion technicians who are still alive, maybe we could figure out how to reverse the process. I'd certainly be willing to be the guinea pig."

Still Diana said nothing, but a small smile drifted across her face.

Juliet opened her eyes and looked at the other woman. "But more than that," she said, "are all those people in positions of power back on Earth who have been converted." She pulled herself more erect in her chair. "God knows what kind of state they're in now, without you and other Visitors to give them instruction."

Diana's soft smile became broader, more smug.

"In a way," Julie went on, "you may have achieved the destruction of our world after all, even though the doomsday device was disarmed. With most of our leaders converted, our governments might collapse, our economy crumble, our military destroy itself or start senseless wars. And so it seems to me that learning how to deconvert people is our highest priority." She slouched down in her chair again, and her gaze turned inward.

"It will take a long time," Julie murmured, as if to herself. "The only facility we have is aboard this ship. Some of the converted might resist. We don't even know who all of them are." Her eyes closed again. She didn't see Diana get out of her chair and come to the crystal wall directly opposite her.

"You could help us," Julie said softly. "You know so much about life, about the mind. You could teach us not to hate you and your people."

Diana didn't speak, but concentrated her thoughts. As when she had forced Julie to let her escape, she spoke directly into the human woman's mind.

I can *help*, she said silently. *If you'll let me*.

"We don't have to be enemies," Julie murmured. "We could share. If only you'd offered to share instead of trying to steal our water, our lives."

I'm sorry about that, Diana said directly into Julie's mind. *I'd like to help you, but I can't do it in prison.*

"How can we trust you?" Juliet asked. Her voice was low and flat, as if she were in some kind of trance. "Martin, yes, and the other fifth columnists—we can trust them, but there are so many, many others."

They would follow me, Diana thought. *Even Martin would, if he knew that I was on your side.*

"Without your help," Julie said, "our world will take years to recover, decades, if at all. You could shorten that time, assure its reality."

Yes, I could do that. But first, I have to be free. You can let me out of here, Julie. You can convince Mike Donovan that I'm on your side. Do that, Julie. Let me help you.

Julie opened her eyes. They were glazed, staring into unknown depths. "I'll need a torch," she said, "to cut through the partition."

Yes, that's it, a torch. I'll teach you how to use it, Julie. And then, when I'm free, I'll help you save your world.

Julie sat up, climbed clumsily to her feet. Her eyes did not see. She turned away from Diana and walked slowly to the door. Her hand went up to press the release button, but instead of touching the button with her finger, she covered it with her whole hand. The door did not open. She stood there, leaning against the wall, as if needing support. Then slowly she turned back to Diana. Her eyes cleared, and a smile crossed her face.

"That was very informative," she said, and this time her voice was loud and clear. Diana's smug smile vanished in a scowl of apprehension. "You did this to me before," Julie went on, "when I let you escape. And that tells me something very interesting."

"You know nothing," Diana snarled, "nothing at all."

"Oh, but I do. Though I don't yet know how it works, I know a secret. You can control converted people by telepathy. Just the knowledge that telepathic control exists is significant. Who knows what we can do with that, once we figure it out."

"It won't do you any good," Diana said. "I'm the one who

converted you. I'm the only one who can speak with you that way."

"We'll see," Julie said. "I'll ask Martin to perform a little experiment with me. If it works with him, we may have found our key to recovery." She smiled broadly, and while Diana glowered, pushed the button and went out the door.

Juliet Parrish lay back in a large, comfortable lounge chair in a cabin that they had chosen for the experiment. Martin sat on a stool in front of her while Mike Donovan and Barbara stood on either side of him.

"I'm sorry," Julie said, opening her eyes, "it's just not going to work."

"Dammit," Martin said, "I don't see why not. There's nothing special about Diana except her knowledge. If she could communicate with you telepathically, I should be able to too."

"It's not your fault," Barbara said. "I think Julie's just too tired."

"But isn't that how Diana was able to do it in the first place?" Mike asked.

"No, I *was* tired then, but I was faking most of it. In a way, I suspect it's like hypnotism. That doesn't work if you're tired either, or if you're drunk or distracted or have too low an IQ." She sat up, stretched, then rubbed her eyes. "Right now I feel like I'm all of that."

"I still don't like the fact that you let yourself be used as a guinea pig," Mike said.

"So, who else was going to do it?" Julie countered. "I'm the only one here who's gone through the conversion process."

"But what if you'd underestimated Diana's power?" Donovan insisted. "She was able to make you let her escape before."

"But then," Juliet said, "I didn't know what she was doing. This time I put myself into her hands deliberately, fooled her into thinking she could do it again."

"And could she have?" Martin asked.

"Again, it's like hypnotism. If she told me to do something that I wanted to do anyway or convinced me it would please me to do it or fooled me into not knowing what I was doing, yes, I think she could have controlled me. But in another way it's not hypnotism at all. There's no trance. Just thoughts set into your mind, so that you don't know what's yours and what comes from outside. I knew exactly what I wanted to do, and nothing she could say could have confused me about that.''

"I see what you're getting at," Barbara said. "And that means that your senators, your governors, your generals who were all converted will be controllable by even the subtlest suggestions.''

"Exactly. Since they won't know they *are* being controlled, they can't resist. And since they're confused anyway as a result of the conversion, they're not likely to figure it out for themselves.''

"This is a phenomenon I've never heard of before," Martin said, "but I suspect that, even without telepathy, the control could be exerted by simple suggestion.''

"The Visitors who were controlling people might not even know they were using telepathy," Julie said. "We may not need to be able to learn the technique, but it would surely be a help. In any event, we need to know more." She turned to Barbara. "We need to screen the conversion technicians," she said. "Diana may not be willing to help us, but one of them might.''

"I'll have somebody check the crew roster right away," Barbara said, "but right now, *you* need some sleep.''

"I'm not going to argue with you," Julie said with a yawn.

"This could be a big breakthrough," Sancho Gomez said to William. They were outside the locked compartment where a number of conversion technicians were being held prisoner. William carried the list of those they were going to question.

"Conversion must be an awful thing," William said. "At home, it is used to turn political prisoners into willing workers.''

Just then two fifth columnists, Tim and Ralph, came up the corridor toward them.

"You two make sure nobody causes any trouble in here,''

Sancho told them. Then he unlocked the door and went in. William and the two male guards followed him.

Inside, William called out names, and those who answered he directed to stand to one side. When he finished, there were seventeen technicians out of the fifty or so Visitors present.

"Put those others in a back room," Sancho told the guards. The prisoners, not wanting any trouble, began to comply. The fifth columnist Tim closed the door on them while Ralph stood watch at the corridor.

"It's like this," Sancho said. "You're all highly trained; you all know about the conversion process. What we need is to know how to deconvert people, make them normal again. Can that be done?"

"No real problem," one of the technicians said, "provided the convertee hasn't been damaged in the process."

"We're not going to worry about that," Sancho said. "Not now anyway. But you know that when we get back to Earth, you're not going to be very popular." The technicians, about half men, half women, shuffled uneasily. "But anyone who helps us, well, we'll try to treat you like friends instead of enemies."

"How can you ask us to collaborate with you?" one of the men, a technician named Philip, asked. "Our world is dying. We were only trying to survive."

"Okay," Sancho said, "so you can stay here. But don't you see, we can help you if we can just get on our feet again."

"You'd give us your water?"

"Man, we've got ice caps we don't know what to do with. We've got lots of water, that's no problem. If you had been straight with us instead of trying to cheat us, we could have helped you. So okay, we still can, but we've got to make sure our mayors and presidents are okay first. Can you understand it?"

"You accuse us of betrayal," a woman named Lucy said, "but how do we know you won't betray us in return?"

"And you," Sancho Gomez said, "asked us to take you on faith. So now I'm asking you to take us on faith."

"I think we owe it to them, Kyle," a second man told his companion. "They don't want their world to die any more than we want ours to die, and we tried to kill them all."

"No way," Kyle said. "They may *look* like people—sort of—but they're just *relavish*. Count me out."

"Hey, you lizard," Sancho said. "I know what that word means. What it *really* means is that your mind is small. You're afraid of me. You think you're something special. Well, maybe you are, but it's you who's locked up in this room, not me. You want out? Then try being a little more friendly."

The technician turned away.

"I'll help," someone said from the back of the group.

"Okay," Sancho said as the man came forward. "Who are you?"

"Arnold," the technician said.

William looked at his list. "He's a specialist in feedback and deep-mind probing," he told the rebel.

"Sounds like just the guy we need," Sancho said. "Okay, Arnold, let's go talk to Martin. If you behave yourself, we could become good friends."

With Arnold between them, Sancho and William left the compartment. The two fifth columnists backed out and closed the door behind them.

"How about some lunch, Tim," one said. "Come along?"

"Not right now, Ralph," Tim said. "I'm going to get some shut-eye. Haven't slept in twenty hours."

"Okay, I'll see you later." Ralph went off in one direction, and Tim started in the other, but when Ralph was out of sight, Tim came back to the compartment door and stepped inside.

The technicians, and a few of the others who'd come back from the other room, looked up apprehensively. "Kyle," Tim said. "Philip, Lucy, come with me." He drew his pistol and stepped aside to let them precede him out the door. When the door closed behind him, he holstered his gun.

"I liked the way you talked in there," he said. "You sound just like the kind of people we need."

"There's an underground?" Philip asked.

"You've got it. Our race against theirs. We'll work out a story later, so you can go back in there and find more supporters. Right now I want to take you to Gretchen. We're working on a plan to free Diana."

Chapter 7

"The telepathic effect was an unexpected by-product," Arnold was explaining to Martin. They were sitting to one side of the command center. William and Sancho had returned to their quarters for some much needed rest, but Caleb Taylor, Maggie Blodgett, and the medical assistant Aaron were sitting in on the interview. "We discovered it," Arnold went on, "only a month or so ago. Diana was extremely interested, to say the least, and had set up a series of experiments, but we had time to run only a few of them."

"Can anybody do that?" Caleb asked. "Give telepathic commands to a convertee?"

"Anybody with a strong enough personality," Arnold said, "which Diana certainly has. As far as we can tell, it works only one way, and only across racial lines. That is, one of us can send to a human convertee, and a human can send to one of us. Convertees can only receive, as far as we know."

"People have been trying to prove the existance of psi powers for years," Maggie Blodgett said. "Just think of what we could do with it if we could induce the ability without actually converting people's minds."

"I don't know that I want anybody reading my mind," Caleb said.

"It really doesn't work that way," Arnold said. "You can't

75

'read' somebody, only pick up their sending. At least as far as we know. And we really don't know much at all about it."

"A most promising line of investigation nonetheless," Aaron agreed. "But we'll have to save that for later. Right now we need to be able to reverse the conversion process. I take it that's possible?"

"It's not often done," Arnold said, "and certainly the deconversion won't be perfect, but, yes, we can reverse most of the effects."

"That's all we need to know," Caleb said. "And you'll teach us how to use the equipment?"

"It's the least I can do. The ecological disaster that's destroying our planet was our own doing. We have no right to destroy your world too."

"I'm glad you see it that way," Martin said. "I hope that we'll be able to save our world anyway once we—"

"Martin!" Peter called from the command center's entrance. "We've got trouble. A group of trustees have turned and are attacking Diana's prison. They're trying to set her free."

The side corridor off which Diana's prison was located joined at right angles a larger corridor down which Caleb Taylor, Maggie Blodgett, and Peter were now running. Arnold and Aaron had stayed behind to call other fifth columnists and rebels to help thwart the escape attempt.

As the entrance to the side corridor came in sight, the group slowed, drew their sidearms, and approached with hasty caution. They could hear the whining sound of a power drill. Hoping the noise would cover their approach, they turned into the corridor entrance to see a number of turncoats, several working the large device at Diana's door, the rest facing them with drawn weapons.

Wild and explosive shots flashed from both sides. Peter received a small wound, but the others were able to duck back around the corner. Their own fire had been ineffective.

Caleb and Martin tried to maneuver into a position from which they could see down the corridor, but the turncoats' fire kept them ducking. Even Martin's crack marksmanship was ineffective here.

Aaron came up from behind them with word that other rebels and fifth columnists would soon be joining them, even as the support party appeared at the other end of the main corridor.

The turncoats must have heard them, because a sudden fusillade of fire blazed out from the corridor entrance.

"We've got to get to them from the other side," Caleb cried.

"Then we'll be shooting at each other," Martin said. He gestured to the reinforcements at the other side of the corridor entrance. Meanwhile, the sound of the drill went on, now changing in pitch as it began to bite into the material of Diana's prison door.

When Martin had everybody's attention, he signaled for a cease-fire. The turncoats continued to shoot, making enough noise to obscure most of his words, but he relied on gestures to convey his plan. He set Peter facedown on the deck, close to the corner, with Maggie Blodgett kneeling beside him, then Aaron standing next to her, and indicated that the rebels and fifth columnists on the other side of the entrance arrange themselves similarly. Using his hands, he showed them just what he wanted them to do when he gave the signal. Then they waited.

The turncoats stopped firing after a moment. After all, no target had presented itself for some time. The whine of the drill continued. It was now the only noise in the corridor. When Martin felt he had let the turncoats stew long enough, he gave his signal. The six fighters lying, kneeling, or standing by either corner moved in unison, having completely clear lines of fire as they turned their respective corners. Then he and Caleb, and two rebels from the other side, stepped full into the entrance.

Their timing was perfect, their volley decimating. Tense and unnerved at the long silence, the turncoats were taken unprepared, though they faced Martin and his people with drawn guns. Four turncoats went down, the drill was struck and rendered inoperative, and four others, who had been behind the bulky device, managed to escape but not without wounds.

The battle was over as quickly as that. Three of the fallen turncoats were dead, but the fourth, Tim, who had been in the fifth column almost since the beginning, was still alive, though mortally wounded.

Aaron knelt beside the dying Visitor. "Why did you do it?" he asked while Maggie Blodgett and Martin looked on.

"We are the people," Tim said. "These others," he waved a weak but disparaging hand, "they are just cattle."

"You know that's not true," Aaron said. "Mammal or reptile, we share a common intelligence."

"No," Tim insisted, though his voice was weak. "Our two races can never find a common ground. And we'll win, Aaron. The eight of us were not the only ones who have seen the truth. There are others—among the trustees, locked in compartments, even among the fifth column, as I was."

"How can you hope to win?" Maggie asked. "There are so few of you, and you're not soldiers."

"*You* were few," Tim said. "*You* were not soldiers, yet you drove us away. You defeated a force of fifty ships. The odds are about the same now, only it is we, the truly loyal, who will prevail this time."

"No," Aaron said. "We won't let it happen." But his words were wasted. A thin stream of green blood trickled out of Tim's mouth as the Visitor died.

"But it could happen," Martin said. He squatted down on his heels, and then sat on the deck. "We don't know who to trust, they can get to us any time."

"Lock everybody up," Maggie suggested.

"Then who would run the ship?" Martin asked.

"Well, not you, for one," Aaron said. "You haven't slept since long before we came on board."

"I'll be all right," Martin insisted, though his resonant voice was oddly hoarse and ragged.

"Two hours' sleep," Aaron insisted. He stood and Maggie helped him bring Martin to his feet. The fifth column leader was too weak to resist. He was already half asleep as it was. Maggie and Aaron half carried, half walked him along the corridors till they came to a medical lab.

"Put him on that cot," Aaron said. "I'll get a sedative."

Martin sat on the edge of the hospital cot, but when Maggie tried to get him to lie down, he pushed her away. He was staring at a strange chair set into an alcove in the far wall.

"Why didn't I think of it before?" he said, and forced himself to his feet.

"Martin," Maggie said, "please, you're going to kill yourself."

"But don't you see?" Martin said. "This is where Diana gave Mike Donovan the truth serum that made him reveal that I was his contact to the fifth column."

"Truth serum?" Aaron asked. He was carrying a flat device with a pistol-grip handle, a hypodermic that needed no needle.

"Yes," Martin said. "Truth serum. It took a lot to work on Mike, but it should be a lot more effective on us."

Martin lay on the hospital cot, sound asleep, completely oblivious to the activity going on around him. Mike Donovan and Juliet Parrish had been summoned and had come to witness the experiment. Caleb and Elias Taylor had brought in three trustees without having told them the purpose of this experiment, and Barbara joined them as Maggie Blodgett and Aaron put the first of them, a woman named Jennifer, into the alcove chair.

"Do you have any idea how much Diana used on you?" Aaron asked Mike. He was holding the syringe device that held the truth serum.

"All I know is that she shot me with it twice."

"It's set for twenty, but then she'd have to compensate for your differing metabolism and body chemistry." He turned the knob on the syringe. "I'll try it at five first."

Under questioning, the trustee admitted some reservation but seemed to be sympathetic to the humans' cause.

"That's not conclusive," Julie said. "She could be agreeing with us just to throw us off."

"I know," Aaron said. "Maybe we ought to test one of us, like Barbara or myself."

"Let's go ahead and run these other two through first," Elias suggested. He pushed the male Visitor he was holding over to the chair while Maggie helped Jennifer to a cot.

"What is your name?" Aaron asked the Visitor after giving the injection.

"Kyle," the Visitor said.

"Are you human or Visitor?" Mike asked.

"I'm a Visitor," Kyle answered.

"How do you feel about humans?"

"I hate them," Kyle said. He showed no signs of resistance, simply stated his feelings.

"You're a trustee," Aaron said. "You said you'd obey Martin's orders, isn't that right?"

"That's right," Kyle said. His voice was becoming slurred, and his head was shaking slightly.

"That's not a good question," Caleb said. "He's been telling the truth about what he told Martin, but he could have been lying then."

"All right," Aaron said. He paused a moment, then asked Kyle one more question. "Whose side are you on, Martin's or Diana's?"

"Diana's," Kyle said.

"He's going to pass out in a minute," Aaron said.

"Jennifer already has," Maggie told them. "You'd better use less next time."

"I'll set it for three."

Caleb Taylor brought the third trustee forward. "No," Aaron said. "I'm next." And he shot the dose into his own neck.

"Why did you do that?" Donovan asked, alarmed.

"To prove myself," Aaron said, moving to sit in the alcove chair.

"But surely you don't think we doubt you?" Julie asked.

"No, I don't think that." His eyes got a bit out of focus.

"Hey, come on," Elias said. "This is a good test, he'll cooperate. Say Aaron, what color is your skin?"

"Green," Aaron said.

"Have you ever eaten a human?"

"No."

"What do you think of your Leader?"

"He's a tyrant and a monster."

"Have you been keeping a secret from us?"

"Yes."

"What is it?"

"I was Diana's lover for a while."

* * *

The plan was actually quite simple. After Aaron recovered from his injection and Martin awoke, they all discussed how to proceed. It was decided that all the fifth columnists without exception would be tested first. That would encourage the cooperation of the trustees and the other Visitors who were now being kept prisoner. In each case, someone who knew the subject would ask a question the answer to which the subject would rather not be known. If they passed that test, then the rest of their answers could probably be trusted. After that, the trustees would be tested, and those who didn't pass would be weeded out. Any who refused would be assumed to be enemies.

That agreed upon, Barbara volunteered to be the next to undergo the ordeal. She passed with flying colors, as did Martin and Peter, much to everyone's relief. Caleb Taylor was just bringing in the first group of fifth columnists when Sancho Gomez came bursting in.

"Those damn bastards somehow got guns," he said.

"Who?" Mike Donovan demanded.

"I don't know, but they're shooting at us. William's been hurt."

"We can't *fight*," Robert Maxwell said, pacing up and down the conference room. "We can't go *home*." Though it was still some hours before dawn, all the rebels were awake and present. "And we can't sit still any longer. What are we going to do?"

"I got a message from Linda at the lighthouse, just a few minutes ago," Claire Bryant said. "They're having the same problem, only worse, because of the Visitor technicians with them. At least they all have the antitoxin now, so they don't have to wear their respirators, but there's a problem with providing them with live food."

"Pet stores," Robert said. "Haven't they thought of that?"

"Well, yes," Claire said, "but they've bought out all the rats, mice, hamsters, guinea pigs, parakeets, and even kittens and rabbits in the stores in their area."

"Not kittens too," Paul Overbloom cried.

"Well, that was what was left."

"How about snakes and lizards?" came a voice from the door. It was Ham Tyler, with Chris Faber right behind him.

"Thank God you're back," Robert said, rushing over to pump his hand and pound his shoulder. "We still haven't heard any word from the ship."

"I think we can write them off," Ham said. "We're going to have plenty enough problems as it is."

"You've talked with the network. What do they have to say?"

"Nothing very good." He came into the room. All the rebels gave him their attention. "From one source or another, I've learned that the President, Vice President, the entire cabinet, and the most influential members of both houses of Congress have probably been converted. Federal government is at a standstill. Local government isn't much better. Dammit, there were an awful lot of official visits to the Mother Ship over the last year. Every one of them is suspect. And the real problem is that two hundred fifty million people out there, almost the entire population of this country, aren't even aware of it."

"It's the most bizarre situation in the world," Chris put in. "You go out on the street, and if you don't know what's going on, it looks like business as usual. Prices are coming down, products are available again. Ask anybody and they'll tell you that we'll be back to normal within a month."

"It's the same the world over," Ham said. "I'd never thought I'd pity Russia, but their bureaucracy is bigger than ours, and so they're hurting a lot worse. Places where the government is relatively weak are doing a lot better."

"How about our Lieutenant Governor?" Fred Linker asked.

"Dennis Simon? He spent three days on the Mother Ship. I don't think there's any question but that he's converted. You must have heard some of his broadcasts yesterday."

"We did," Robert Maxwell said. "Martial law continues in effect—for two weeks, he says, for whatever that's worth."

"Nothing," the Fixer said. "We're going to see these United States become disunited, each state for itself, a hodgepodge of neofascists. Those Visitors did more damage than even *they* knew."

"So what are we going to do about it?" Claire asked.

"What *can* we do?" Ham asked back. "If we could deconvert people, if we could somehow get people to believe that their elected officials *have* been converted, we might have some chance. But without Donovan and Julie, and the ship, I don't see what we can do. Dammit, this isn't my line of business. I *start* wars, not finish them."

"Hold on, you guys," somebody called from the back of the room. "We've got another special announcement."

"I've had enough of special announcements," Robert shouted.

"I think you'll like this one," was the response. "It's Julie."

Everyone's attention became riveted on the screen.

"To all the people of the world," Juliet Parrish was saying, "and especially to the people of Los Angeles. I am speaking to you from a Visitor Mother Ship. It is in our control, and we are returning to Earth. Among us are a large number of Visitors. Most of these people bear only feelings of strong friendship with us. As has happened too many times in our own past, they were victims of an evil government and are not evil in and of themselves. I hope that you will be tolerant during the days and months to come. We have much to learn from them, and this time, instead of empty promises, their knowledge will be ours.

"More importantly," she continued, "we bear with us in the holds of this ship ten thousand living human beings, captives of the Visitors, held in suspended animation. Your neighbors, your friends, your loved ones. Without the assistance of hundreds of Visitor technicians, these people cannot be brought back to life. Just as quickly as we can we will be bringing these poor people down to the plant where they were brought when taken from their homes. Please help us return these people to their families.

"And last, we hold a special prisoner ourselves. Diana, the first science officer and second-in-command of the Visitor fleet, is now in a security cell aboard this ship. It is she more than John, more than any other Visitor, who is responsible for the evil that has been done to us. She *will* be brought to justice. She *will* stand trial.

"Shortly, the ship now under our command will once again

float above the skies of Los Angeles. Be assured the enemy has not returned."

Julie's image disappeared to be replaced momentarily by the interrupted scene of the movie that had been playing which, in turn, was replaced by frantic, sleepy-eyed newscasters trying to interpret and explain what had just been said.

"All right," Ham Tyler said, shouting above the noise of the cheers, "now we know what to do."

"But they're back," Maxwell said. "We've won at last."

"Don't count on it," Ham said. "Remember when they tried to arrest us when we were at the plant before? Julie has just told the world where she's going to be. There's plenty of time for those who want to set a trap for her there."

"Mike was right," Robert said. "You're too damn paranoid. How could even the Lieutenant Governor justify an attack on that plant with ten thousand lives at stake?"

"I can think of several ways," Ham said, "and so can he. I don't want to guess, I want to know. They didn't listen to us, and we have no assurance they'll listen to Donovan and Julie. Do you want to just sit back here and take a chance?"

Robert stared at him a moment, then nodded his head in agreement.

"All right," Ham yelled, "let's get a move on."

Chapter 8

Los Angeles, so briefly free of the hovering Mother Ship, was once more in its shadow. Juliet Parrish's message had gone out once every hour, but not everyone had seen it. The timing was wrong. It was early morning, and most people hadn't yet awakened. When they did, and saw the huge disk shape overhead, their spirits were crushed.

From the belly of the Mother Ship, three shuttles emerged. Each was as large as the component design allowed. They descended, drifting east toward the plant north of Pomona.

There, a cordon of police and National Guard stood around the perimeter of the facility. This time, it seemed, they were concerned with keeping people out, rather than with disrupting the activities of the suspension plant. A speaker system aiming outward toward the crowds kept repeating Julie's message. Still, many of the people gathered there did not believe what they heard and shouted curses and threats.

The three shuttles hovered over the plant from which so many human victims had been taken. Inside the wire fence was a contingent of National Guard under the command of Colonel Kent Fletcher. The soldiers moved aside as the first of the shuttles descended to the paved yard of the plant. The second landed moments later, and then the third. When all three were down, the hatches opened.

From the shuttle nearest the plant came a wary and armed

Mike Donovan and Julie Parrish, immediately followed by Martin and Barbara and, between them, Diana, her hands bound by strange cuffs. From the other ships came rebels, followed by fifth columnists, and then a steady stream of translucent white plastic coffins. Under the supervision of rebels and Visitors, these began to come from the first shuttle too.

Colonel Fletcher stood waiting for a moment. The two captains and two lieutenants who made up his staff watched nervously as the rebels and their prisoner approached. Then the colonel squared his shoulders and marched forward to greet the victors, his staff close behind.

They stopped when they were just two paces apart. Mike, having gotten word from Robert about the troubles there earlier, was apprehensive. Colonel Fletcher, however, saluted sharply, then stepped forward to shake his hand.

"Mr. Donovan," he said, "it's a pleasure to meet you at last. Miss Parrish . . ." He offered her his hand. "You have accomplished a miracle." He looked from Martin to Barbara and back. "I never thought I'd say this," he said, "but if you're in any way responsible for bringing these people back, I'm glad to meet you." He shook hands with each and then stepped back.

"I take it," Mike said, "that not all those people out there are quite so pleased."

"Indeed they are not," Colonel Fletcher said. "Most of them did not see your broadcast, and a good number of them don't care. They thought the Visitors were gone forever, and then to have that ship come back again—" he gestured to where it hung in the sky, "—well, it's been hard for them to accept."

"That was one of the things we were worried about," Juliet said.

"How many captives have you brought back?" the colonel asked. His staff stood silently to either side and slightly behind him.

"On this trip," Mike said, "just a hundred and fifty. They are our first concern, of course, but not our only one." He stepped aside and glanced at Martin and Barbara, who pushed Diana forward to face the colonel.

"Ah, Diana," the colonel said. "How happy I am to see you." He clasped his hands behind his back. "You can be sure," he said to Mike Donovan, "that we'll take very good care of her. And of the other Visitors too."

"You understand," Mike said, "that the Visitors we brought down with us are not only our friends, but have much to offer. The process by which those people," he gestured to the continuing stream of coffinlike containers, "have been put into suspended animation can be of great value to us."

"Are all of these aliens, then, necessary to the unprocessing of these poor people?"

"No," Martin said. "Most of them are just workers, or else drawn from other disciplines where they are not needed. We have left several trusted people in charge of the ship. There are approximately two thousand more of them up there, confined to their quarters until we can prove their trustworthiness."

"I see," said the colonel. He did not seem overly pleased. "And children too?" He was looking past them to where Elizabeth stood at the hatch of the shuttle.

"Just the one child," Mike said. "She had been taken up to the ship some time before we captured it. We're bringing her back to her father."

"The most important thing," Juliet said, "is not to revive these people, but to try to identify and cure those who have been converted."

"I don't understand," Colonel Fletcher said.

"We have every reason to believe," Barbara explained, "that most of your government officials underwent a kind of brainwashing process while on a visit to our ship. We think we can reverse that process."

"I see," the colonel repeated. His pleasure seemed to be diminishing rapidly.

"We've begun the process of testing all the Visitors left on board the ship," Mike Donovan said, "to find out which ones we can trust. A large percentage of them are highly trained technicians, engineers, scientific specialists. They are all willing to give us the information and knowledge that John, their Supreme Commander, once promised us."

"That's good," Colonel Fletcher said with a singular lack of enthusiasm. "It would be nice to come out of this mess with something to show for it."

Mike and Julie exchanged glances. Something was going wrong, and they had no idea what it was.

"Perhaps," the colonel went on, "we ought to go inside and see how things are going there."

"All right," Donovan said, and as a group they entered the plant. Elizabeth followed along behind.

There the last of the coffins were being stacked to one side while Visitor technicians were opening up the service panels on the processing equipment. There were also a number of police and Guardsmen standing at attention, carefully out of the way.

"How many more humans are on board the ship?" the colonel asked.

"Approximately nine thousand eight hundred and fifty," Julie said, "but the entire rebel invading force is here with us."

"About these in the coffins: do they have to be unprocessed immediately?"

"Those on board the ship," Martin said, "can probably be left alone for quite awhile. They're connected to special life-support systems to keep them—uh—fresh. But these here will have to be tended to within a few days, or they'll die."

"I see," Colonel Fletcher said. "But they don't need immediate attention?"

"No, but the longer they stay without support, the greater the chance that they won't survive revitalization."

"Very good," the colonel said. "In that case we have plenty of time." He cleared his throat with a loud "harrumph," and the police and Guardsmen all drew their weapons. "You're all under arrest."

"What the hell's going on?" Mike Donovan shouted. Most of the Visitors in the plant were not armed, but neither those who were nor the rebels dared go for their weapons.

"You don't expect me to believe," the colonel said with heavy sarcasm, "that these *people*," he waved at the Visitor technicians, "would actually join you against their own kind."

"Of course we do," Julie said angrily. "They've chosen a higher loyalty than just to their own race." Around her, police and Guardsmen were relieving the rebels and fifth columnists of their weapons.

"No," Colonel Fletcher said, "I don't accept that. I know about conversion. You've all spent a lot of time aboard the aliens' ship. Obviously there's some kind of plot, and you and these aliens are in it together."

"That's not true," Barbara said.

"You expect me to believe *you*," the colonel snapped. "Nonsense. You've hatched a plan to salvage what you can of a bad situation."

"You're making a big mistake," Mike said.

"That's what they all say," the colonel responded. "I can't trust any of you, and I'm going to put you someplace safe until I can learn the truth."

"But what about the rest of the people on the ship?" Julie said.

"Mr. Donovan here," the colonel said, "figured out how to fly a shuttle. I think I have some men in my command who are equally capable. We'll bring the rest of the human prisoners down and unprocess them ourselves. The Visitors still on the ship can stay there. But you, my friends, are going to be put away for a while."

He gave a command to one of the soldiers, who went to the sliding double doors and opened them. Six security wagons pulled into the plant, and under the colonel's supervision the rebels and Visitors were loaded inside. Then the paddy wagons drove off into the early morning.

Ham Tyler and Chris Faber crouched behind a pile of discarded truck tires among a field of similar such piles. They were a few hundred feet from the fence surrounding the Visitor's suspended-animation plant. On their right were Robert Maxwell and Claire Bryant, and beyond them were half a dozen more rebels. Fred Linker, Paul Overbloom, and the rest of the rebels were on Ham's left. All had a good view of the plant, of the angry and curious people closer to the fence, of the police and National Guardsmen inside—and of the security vans now being loaded with their friends.

"What are we going to do?" Robert whispered loudly. "We can't just let them be taken away."

"You want to launch an attack," Ham whispered back, "I'll

cover your rear." They had arrived an hour before, found the police and Guardsmen already in place, and had witnessed the arrival of the three shuttles. When Juliet Parrish, Mike Donovan, Martin, and Barbara had met the colonel and his staff, several of the rebels had wanted to come out of hiding and join their fellows. It had taken all Ham's authority to keep them concealed.

"Going up against the Visitors is one thing," Fred said, "but I don't like shooting up my own people."

"You'd never make it, in any event," Ham said. "Colonel Fletcher, the one in charge, has a reputation for maintaining his people in top fighting form."

The rebels murmured among themselves, passing back and forth their observations and comments. And then when the security vans drove away, it was too late to do anything.

At the plant the Guardsmen took up positions in and near the building while the police went back to the problem of dispersing the crowd. With the rebels and Visitors gone, they had more success than before. Ham decided that now was the time to fall back, before they were discovered.

Reluctantly, almost ashamedly, the rebels returned to their trucks. Ham took Fred aside and led him to one of the smaller vehicles, a step van with a plumbing company sign painted on the side.

"Take two others," he said, "and find out where Mike and the others are being taken. I have a feeling it won't be to a regular security installation."

Fred nodded, called two friends, and drove off before the National Guard vans could get out of sight.

"I can't understand it," Robert Maxwell said. "They should have been welcomed as heroes."

"I'll lay you odds," Ham Tyler answered, "that whoever issued the orders has been converted."

"That whole crowd of civilians around the plant hasn't been converted," Claire said. "They just don't like the idea of that Mother Ship being overhead again."

"Julie should have stayed in orbit longer," Paul Overbloom said. "Nobody watches TV at that hour of the morning. They should have broadcast their message for a whole day before coming down."

"That might have helped," Ham agreed, "but most people do what they're told most of the time, even if what they're told doesn't make much sense. And the people who are telling them what to do are soft-headed because of what the Visitors did to them. So we'd still have trouble even if Julie's message had gone out for a week."

"Are we going to try to rescue them?" Claire Bryant asked.

"There aren't enough of us," Robert said. "Even if we bring in people from the lighthouse."

"All right," Ham decided, "it's obvious we need more help. Chris, see if you can round up any other rebel groups who might be in the area. Maxwell, you're still in charge of the San Pedro group. Get everybody ready and leave only a skeleton crew at the lighthouse, just enough to take care of the children."

"And what are you going to do?" Robert asked.

"Get back into the network and find out more about who ordered that arrest and why. I might be able to apply a little pressure and have the order countermanded." His smile indicated that the kind of pressure he had in mind would result in dead bodies. "And if I can't do that, I want to at least find out what they intend to do with our people. Because we *are* going to rescue them, one way or another."

It was not, in fact, a standard security facility to which Julie, Mike, the other rebels, and the fifth columnists were taken. It was instead an abandoned private sanitarium on the coast just beyond Laguna Beach. The single huge building was surrounded by a ten-foot-high stone wall, with broken glass set into the top and a single gate on the landward side. Toward the ocean, the wall abutted the rear of the building, with its windows giving an excellent view of the bluff on which the sanitarium stood and of the beach below.

There was plenty of room in the walled courtyard for all the security vans and the motorcycle escort. The Guardsmen supervised the unloading, leading the prisoners in small groups, human and Visitor, from the vans to the double front doors. When one van was emptied, the driver pulled it around to the side of the building, and the next was driven into place.

Mike Donovan, Juliet Parrish, Barbara, Martin, Diana, and Elizabeth Maxwell were among the last to be unloaded. The Guardsmen were terse and efficient but not rough with them as they helped them down from the van and led them up the stairs to the sanitarium. Colonel Fletcher and one of his lieutenants fell in beside them as they entered the building.

"Why are we being brought here?" Donovan demanded.

"For two reasons," the colonel answered. "First, you are a special problem. We can't put you in among regular prisoners. We don't have facilities for this many in private cells unless we spread you out all over the state. Your Visitor friends wouldn't live very long in a regular jail or prison. Even your lives would be in danger.

"And second, this place is very secure. Until it went broke two years ago, only the most dangerous, the most violent psychotics were kept here, people who could escape from almost every other sanitarium. The security is excellent."

The main lobby was dusty with disuse but seemed to be fully furnished. As the prisoners were brought in, they were segregated by race. The humans were led off to the right wing, the Visitors to the left.

"What about this little girl," a Guardsman asked as Elizabeth was brought up.

"She doesn't belong with these people," Colonel Fletcher said. "Can you take care of her until we locate her family?"

"Should be no problem," another Guardsman said. "We've got plenty of room in back. She can play with some of the physical therapy stuff the doctors left behind."

"How are you going to feed us?" Martin asked when it was his turn.

"You get your meals like everybody else," the colonel said.

"The Visitors can't eat our food," Juliet told him. "Only live animals or freshly killed meat."

The colonel looked from Martin to Barbara with growing distaste. "And to think I shook hands with you. But I suppose you're too valuable to let starve. Lieutenant Casey?"

"Yes, sir," his staff officer said.

"You heard the lady. See to it these Visitors are fed 'properly.'"

"Yes, sir," Casey said.

* * *

Mike and Julie, following the rest of the rebels, were led down a short hall at the end of which was a heavy fire door. Beyond this was another hall, elling to the right along the back of the building. The walls of both sides of this corridor were mostly heavy reinforced glass, allowing complete visibility into the rooms beyond. Doors of a similar glass were set between the windows, each with a large, complicated lock.

The first rooms were small and looked like individual cells. Other rooms held various kinds of therapy equipment. Near the end on the right were two large rooms, similarly windowed, each with a set of bunks, chairs, and a few tables. Across from them were four smaller rooms in which interviews might be conducted. At the very end of the hall was what looked like a common room, but they didn't go in there. Instead, they were let into one of the bunk rooms where the rest of the rebels were already assembled. Two doors connecting the two bunk rooms were left open.

"Looks like they got us this time," Elias Taylor said. He was trying to sound devil-may-care, but wasn't pulling it off too well. His father, Caleb, was standing at one of the outside windows, looking out into the courtyard at the front of the building.

"It's better than some of the jails I've been in," Sancho Gomez said. "Only problem is, no bathrooms."

"There's one down the corridor," Maggie Blodgett told him. "I saw it when I came by. Not much privacy, though, same glass wall in front."

"What happened to Elizabeth?" Caleb asked, turning from the window.

"She's staying with the guards," Juliet said. "They're not bad men—they'll take care of her."

The other rebels, seven altogether, sat listlessly in chairs, looked out windows, or glared through the glass wall at the guards in the corridor. Then one, a short, stocky Oriental named Thomas Lee, got up from his chair, picked it up, and smashed it against the outside window nearest him. The heavy chair just bounced off the reinforced glass. The guard outside watched impassively. "Goddamn bastards," Lee swore, and swung the chair again. He succeeded in breaking one leg off. The glass was unmarked. Still the guard did nothing.

"I think it's a waste of time," Mike Donovan said, "and if you keep it up, we'll run out of furniture real fast."

"I want to know why we're *in* here," Lee shouted. "*We're* the ones who drove the fleet off. *We're* the ones who captured Diana. We're *heroes*, goddamn it."

"Apparently not everybody thinks so," Julie said dryly. Out in the hall, the guard continued to watch. He seemed almost bored.

They were served a late breakfast on paper plates with plastic utensils which were shoved through a narrow trap at the foot of the door. The food, though not exciting, was relatively hot and decently prepared.

"I think our friend the colonel is acting far too independently," Caleb said around a mouthful of scrambled eggs.

"He's probably been converted," Sancho added.

"I don't think so," Julie said. "I really have only myself to compare with—and Sean, of course—but he seems to be in complete control of himself."

"I think you're right," Mike agreed. "Sean was awfully quiet after he came back from the ship. Things like his not being interested in baseball wouldn't be noticed by anybody who hadn't known him before, of course. But now that I think about it, there were other signs I just didn't want to notice at the time. The colonel is showing none' of those signs at all. God, I hope Sean's all right."

"I'm sure he is," Julie said. "Ham or Robert must have found him at Visitor Headquarters. He's probably safe at the lighthouse right now."

"You know," Thomas Lee said, coming over with a paper cup of coffee, "we don't even know how that raid came out. I'm sure Ham and Chris know their stuff, but we never got any word, and nothing was ever mentioned on TV."

"They're out there somewhere," Mike said. "I just can't see the Fixer failing on a job like that one. And whether they succeeded or not, they must know that something has happened to us. We sure let everybody know where we were going to be."

"They probably walked into a trap," Elias Taylor said, "just like we did."

"What about our friends up on the ship?" Maggie Blodgett asked. "When we don't go back up for another load of canned people, Peter is going to know something is wrong."

"He's going to have his own problems," Donovan said. "First, there are still several turncoats on the loose. I wish we'd taken the time to clear up that mess before landing. And then, what if Colonel Fletcher decides to send his troops up in the shuttles? How's Peter or Aaron or Arnold going to know they aren't friends?"

"Peter can always refuse to let him dock, can't he?" Julie asked.

"Sure, but why should he do that?" Mike asked. "Unless Fletcher does something to make him suspicious. Peter's not dumb, but the trouble is that Peter and the others are not real leaders. Even if they keep Fletcher out, I don't see what they can do about finding us. I was counting on Martin and Barbara taking over after this first trip."

"So it doesn't look like we're going to get any help," Caleb Taylor said. "We can't count on anybody knowing where we are. If we're going to get out of here, we'll have to do it ourselves."

Maggie said, "Our only advantage over the people they kept here before is that we're not crazy."

"I wouldn't be too sure of that," Elias said.

When lunch came, the procedure was different. A Guardsman opened the door, his M-16 drawn, and with two other guards, equally alert, motioned the rebels to go stand over against the far wall. Then two more guards wheeled in carts holding covered trays. While these were being set on a nearby table, the three armed men kept their weapons trained on the rebels.

"Hey," Caleb Taylor called, "why the hell are we being kept locked up?"

"Why shouldn't you be locked up?" A guard with sergeant's

stripes asked. "If it weren't for you and other rebels like you, we would have gotten a lot from the Visitors."

"Like what?" Elias asked.

"Like a cure for cancer, for one thing," the sergeant said.

"They wouldn't have given it to us," Mike Donovan answered. "That was just a false promise to make us want to cooperate."

"That's your idea," the sergeant said. "They never had a chance to give it to us because you guys started causing trouble right from the beginning. Every time John or Diana got ready to release some of their technology to us, you'd pull a raid like that time at the medical center."

"We had to let people know what the Visitors were really like," Julie told him, "what they were really up to. You saw the broadcast."

"Yeah, the one you faked, and the real one too. I don't believe all that fancy makeup stuff you claimed. And besides, my wife could really have used that cancer cure."

"You don't understand," Sancho Gomez started to say.

"I understand well enough," the sergeant insisted as the two carts were wheeled out. The other two armed guards moved toward the door, still keeping their weapons trained on the rebels. The sergeant was the last one out. "I understand you guys are getting better than you deserve," he said from the doorway.

"Now, wait a minute," Maggie Blodgett protested, stepping forward. The sergeant turned the gun on her. "You say we're here because we drove the aliens off. Colonel Fletcher accused us of being collaborators. You can't have it both ways."

"The colonel's got strange ideas. Fortunately for your friends in the other wing, the Lieutenant Governor wants all these aliens kept alive. We'll get what we want out of them. It's just a matter of time."

"You may not have that much time," Juliet Parrish told him. "We don't know how long the antitoxin lasts, but if the Visitors here don't get another dose pretty soon, they'll die just like all the others."

"Not all of them, maybe. That toxin you spread isn't one hundred percent effective, you know. We've got some survivors."

"Survivors?" Mike asked. "Are you sure?"

"Sure I'm sure. Some of them never got exposed, some got hold of some kind of respirator, but some we thought were dead revived after a day or so. Even the strongest pesticide leaves a few bugs alive, you know."

"But then why are you keeping *us*?" Sancho asked.

"Because you're too dangerous. You turn against your own kind, you destroy any chance we might have for learning the alien's technology. But we'll get it, some of it, one way or another. A lot of them have already agreed to cooperate. Those who don't will stand trial with you. Not that that trial will be very fair," he finished with a grin. He stepped back through the doorway and shut it behind him. The sound of the complicated latch locking was unmistakable.

"Damn fool," Mike said. "Can't he see that half of what he says contradicts the other half?"

"Of course he can't," Julie said. "He's not thinking, he's just angry. If there *had* been a cancer cure, and if John *had* given it to us, his wife would be healthy today."

"I think I can see his point," Caleb said, "even if it's wrong. But right now let's eat before this food gets cold."

The presence of the food under the flimsy plastic covers made them all hungry again though they'd eaten not that long ago.

"How can there be survivors?" Maggie wanted to know, trying to cut her ham with the plastic knife.

"Like the man said," Sancho answered, "there are always some bugs that are immune to any poison."

"Unless, of course," Julie offered, "the poison is so broad and powerful that, like strychnine, it just kills everything. Which our toxin wasn't. It was specific to the Visitors and affected their nervous system. Think about Elizabeth—she's naturally immune."

"I like the part about how willing those survivors are to cooperate," Elias Taylor said with a wry laugh. "Hell, I'd be willing to cooperate too if I were in their position—until they gave me a chance to escape."

Caleb said, "I wonder just how long it will take those survivors to figure out that they can influence anybody who's been converted."

"If they're desperate enough," Julie said, "not long. All one of them would have to do would be to *want* a convertee to help them. They'd see that person behaving in an oddly cooperative fashion and know the truth right away."

"And these survivors," Caleb went on, "will be questioned by converted scientists, converted politicians, converted generals. Not all these Visitors are smart—hell, Willie ain't exactly bright—but some of them are, and you can bet they'll figure things out pretty quickly."

"And once they have even a few people under their control," Maggie went on, "they'll have the wedge they need to gain control of the whole country again."

"And every other country too," Thomas Lee agreed.

"It's a sure thing," Donovan said, "that none of those survivors are fifth columnists."

"That's right," Lee said, "and they'll be angry, just like that sergeant was, so even if they *might* have been on our side, they'll all be against us now."

Mike added, "If they can do to our scientists and politicians what Diana did to Julie, then we've got real trouble."

"We've got to let people know about this," Maggie said.

"And to do that," Lee added, "we've got to get out of here."

"Do you think anybody would believe us about telepathic control?" Mike asked. "If I didn't know better, I'd think we were all paranoid."

"Is that any harder to believe than flying saucers?" Julie asked.

"No, but everybody has *seen* flying saucers now," Mike said. "Real ones. But you're the only person with any evidence of mind control. And the way our credibility is now, I wouldn't bet on your convincing a lot of people, even if we had some way to get the message across."

"Besides," Maggie added, "the people we have to really convince are ones who are in power and thus already converted and controlled. Mike didn't want to believe that Sean was converted, and if Julie's conversion had been successful, do you think she'd want to believe that about herself?"

"What are we arguing about?" Sancho Gomez cried. "None of this matters if we can't figure out a way to escape. If we can do that, *then* we can find out whether the convertees will believe us or not.''

"You're right," Julie told him. "We've got to tackle this thing one step at a time. And the first step is to eat, then get some rest. We're all too far behind on our sleep to be able to think clearly."

"Right," Elias agreed. "And if we stay quiet, the guards may stop paying us so much attention." He looked through the glass wall to where a single Guardsman was slowly walking up and down the corridor outside, keeping his eyes on them as he walked.

Chapter 9

The complex of rooms in the wing where the eleven Visitors were being kept was almost a mirror image of those occupied by the rebels. Here, the corridor entrance from the lobby hall was on the right, and the common room was on the left. Like the rebels, the Visitors had been put into a pair of connecting bunk rooms across from which, clearly visible through the glass walls, were interview rooms.

Unlike the rebels, the Visitors had had to do without breakfast while Lieutenant Casey and two privates had gone into Laguna Beach to find a pet store. Also unlike the rebels, they had not had to suffer being watched while they ate. The first time Barbara popped a live hamster into her mouth, the guard had disappeared up the corridor toward the main lobby.

The cardboard animal boxes stood empty on one of the tables now. All the Visitors sat in chairs or lay in bunks except for Diana, who stood at an outside window watching as two Guardsmen patrolled the grounds inside the high wall.

"Why don't you relax, Diana," Martin called to her. He was sitting at the table, fiddling with one of the perforated boxes.

"Relax?" she said sarcastically, turning to face him. "How can I relax?"

"Why not? We're not being treated badly, all things considered."

"We wouldn't be here at all if it weren't for you," Diana

said. "We'd all be safe on our ship, heading back home now. But no, you, all of you, decided that the survival of our planet, of our people, was not as important as helping these *relavish*."

"What we were doing before was wrong," Martin said. Barbara and another Visitor, Joanna, came over to sit with him.

"Indeed," Diana said. "I think you've got it backward. Sure those rodents we had for lunch have a right to try to survive, but we have a right to eat them too. Humans eat meat—if their cattle tried to revolt and break out of their pens, how long do you think it would take the humans to put the rebellion down and slaughter the whole lot of them?"

"But humans aren't cattle," Joanna said. "That's the difference."

"If they can survive on their own strength," Diana said, "fine. But you, you got into the pens with them. You betrayed your own people."

"You're still missing the point," a Visitor named Lawrence said. "If humans were just animals, you'd be right. But in spite of physical differences, they're every bit as much people as we are."

"What we were doing," Joanna went on, "was not that much different from cannibalism."

"Nonsense," Diana said. "Our races are completely different. The proof of our superiority, of our right to exploit them, is the fact that we had the technology to come to them, while they were unable to come to us."

"That argument has been used to justify brutality before," the Visitor named George said.

"To justify *survival*!" Diana insisted. "We're all going to die unless we get new sources of food and water."

"Haven't you ever heard of trade?" Martin asked wryly. "This world has so much water they could give us all we needed. We pretended to offer them technology in exchange for those phony chemicals. What if our offer had been sincere?"

"What if. That doesn't change the fact that you are all traitors—to your Leader, to your race, to your world."

"But loyal to a broader ideal," Barbara insisted.

"So you say, but I wonder. Might it not rather have been the idea that, after you had helped these humans drive most of the rest of us off, you few fifth columnists would be left here, supposedly their friends, with the entire resources of this planet for yourselves?''

"No, Diana," Martin said, "though I can see how the idea might appeal to you. I believed, and I think we all still believe, that we could have saved all of our people, not just a few, if we had only dealt fairly with the humans of Earth."

Diana snorted and went back to look out the window.

"Even after our deceit was found out," Barbara went on, "we might have been able to make amends. It would have taken a lot of effort, but if we had shown good faith, at least helped repair the damage we had caused, they might have helped us after all. But you spoiled it _for_ us."

"_I_ spoiled it," Diana said in honest surprise. "How did _I_ spoil it?"

"By forcing them to use drastic measures to be rid of us. There are some species of animals here that they regard as pests because they breed so quickly and can survive in any environment. Even our environment, as spoiled as it is. But because of the toxin, which came into existence because of your insane breeding experiments with Robin and Brian—oh, yes, didn't you know? Robin had _two_ children, not just one. The second one died. It was from him that Julie and the others developed the toxin that now makes all animal life on this planet poisonous to us."

"If it's so poisonous, how come we're not dead?" Diana demanded.

"Because they also developed an antitoxin," Barbara replied. "Julie gave you a dose when they rescued you from your escape shuttle. The people whose world you tried to destroy saved your life, Diana. How does that feel?"

"If that's true, they saved me so they could make a mockery of me, put me on trial in front of their whole world. Well, it's not going to happen. We're going to get out of here. We've _got_ to get out of here. The animal life might be ruined for us, but there's still the water."

"That's been poisoned too," William said quietly.

"Indeed it has. But you can distill water, purify and filter it, as they do with their own sewage."

The idea had apparently not occurred to the others. There

was a long moment of consternated conversation, and then a striking-looking woman named Phyllis spoke up.

"But what good will it do us?" she said. "We've spoiled every chance we might have had to come to terms with them."

"Maybe we deserve it," Martin said. "Everything we did was a cheat. A lie. Taking intelligent beings for food. It's all part of the same psychology that led us to destroy our fragile environment in the first place. Maybe we deserve to die."

"I am sick of you," Diana sneered. "Traitors, cowards, excuse makers. Maybe *you* deserve to die, but I don't."

She crossed the room to the door and pounded on the glass. After a moment the guard appeared from the direction of the lobby. Diana pounded again. The guard looked at her speculatively a moment, then turned around to call to someone out of sight. Then he came forward to stand across the corridor from the door.

"What are you up to, Diana?" Martin asked.

"I'm going to get out of this room," Diana said, glaring at him.

After a moment Lieutenant Casey and two other soldiers came up the corridor, and on his inaudible instructions, the guard stepped forward and unlocked the door. The two soldiers, their M-16s leveled, stepped into the room.

"Everybody back against the wall," Casey said. The Visitors complied, and while Diana was backing away Casey pointed a finger at her. "You," he said, and she stopped. "What do you want?"

"I think my life is in danger here," she told him, glaring around the room as if defying them to contradict her. No one spoke. "Can you put me in another room where I'll be safe?"

"Quite easily," Casey said wryly. "Will across the hall do?" He indicated one of the interview rooms on the other side of the corridor.

"That will be just fine," Diana said.

Casey stepped aside and motioned Diana to precede him between the two soldiers while the guard unlocked the other door.

"Wait," one of the Visitors said.

Diana turned a cold eye on the woman. "And what do you want, Zenia?"

"I've been thinking about it," she said, "and I think you're right. I'd like to come with you."

"Indeed, and why should I believe you?"

"You shouldn't, I suppose." She looked hopefully at her former superior officer.

Casey, watching Diana, caught her eye and twitched an eyebrow in silent question.

"All right," Diana said. "If that's all right with you, Lieutenant."

"I really couldn't care," Casey said. He and the guard escorted the two women across the corridor to the other room while the soldiers stood watch. When Diana and Zenia were secured, he came back, looked in at the nine remaining visitors, grinned snidely, and locked that door too.

"Now maybe we can get a little rest," Martin said dryly.

The rest of the day had been uneventful for the rebels in their wing of the sanitarium. The only activity had been bathroom trips—the guard had tactfully stood away from the toilet's window wall when any of the women were there—and supper. Otherwise, they had spent their time sleeping. Two things were accomplished by this: first, they would be well rested come nightfall, and second, the guards who patrolled the corridor became awfully bored and hence less observant.

Outside, night was falling. They had asked that the lights be turned off in their own rooms, but the corridor was well lit. Still, the bunks under the outside windows were in deep shadow, which suited them just fine.

They watched as the single guard walked slowly toward the common room end of the corridor, then back toward the lobby end. He wasn't really patrolling, just trying to stay awake. Several times he stretched and yawned.

The rebels all lay on their bunks, but none of them were asleep. Some had drawn the covers over themselves, others just lay on top of the blankets. Out in the corridor the guard made two more transits and then turned into the bathroom.

Elias Taylor had chosen a bunk that was out of sight from the toilet. As soon as the guard went in to relieve himself, Elias rolled out of his bunk, and Sancho Gomez and Caleb Taylor, on either side, stuffed their pillows under his blanket in a crude imitation of his sleeping form.

Without hesitation, Elias crawled across the corridor-illuminated floor to the corridor wall, staying low just in case the guard should come out unexpectedly. He pressed himself close to the wall, below the glass window, effectively out of sight unless the guard should happen to come right up to the window and look straight down. Even then, the shadow of the sill helped to conceal him.

After a moment's hesitation he moved along the base of the wall until he came to the door. There he paused again, this time to take his wallet from his back pocket. Out of this he took a credit card, a short nail file, a bobby pin, and several other makeshift lock picks. Sitting on his hip in order to keep his head well down below the sill of the window, he reached up toward the lock and began to explore it with his devices.

"He's coming," Maggie Blodgett whispered. Her cot was directly opposite the toilet, and she had watched the guard the whole time. Elias immediately stretched himself out flat, pressing as close against the wall as he could. The guard, unselfconsciously zipping his fly, came out and recommenced his slow amble up and back.

After his third round trip, he paused to look in at the silent rebels. Holding his hand over his eyes to cut down the glare on the glass, he peered first at one end of the room, then the other. It apparently did not occur to him to turn the lights back on for the moment it would take him to make his visual inspection.

When he was satisfied that everything in the two rooms was as dull as it had been all day, he walked to the common room at the end of the hall, went inside, and came out dragging a chair, which he propped up against the far wall. He sat down, holding his rifle across his lap, leaned back, tipped his hat forward, and seemed to go to sleep.

The rebels, having spent the whole day practicing the subterfuge, were not about to take chances now. They remained in their cots, silent and still as ever. From his position, the guard could not see many of them directly, but the light from the corridor cast shadows, and those shadows he could see if he were in fact awake.

But that was all right with Elias. He didn't intend to cast any shadows. Quietly, he eased himself back up into a seated position and once again began probing the lock with his odd assortment of devices.

The rebels knew from experience that the glass wall separating them from the corridor was effectively soundproof. Still it was likely that any noise made fiddling with the lock could be heard on the other side. For this reason, Elias tried to be as quiet as he could, and that, along with his unnatural position, hampered him. Once or twice the other rebels could hear tiny clicks or scrapes as Elias tried first one technique, then another. The guard in the hall, however, did not move.

"I can't do it," Elias whispered loudly. "Dammit, this lock's too good."

"Hush," someone whispered. Elias didn't need to be told that the guard had gotten out of his chair.

Stretching and rubbing his eyes, the guard came over toward the window. He paused to look at his watch as if to see how long he'd been asleep. Once again he peered in through the reinforced glass. But this time he apparently decided that he couldn't see well enough, because he unhooked a flashlight from his belt, turned it on, and played the beam over the bunks, one by one. The light passed over Elias's faked bunk, but did not pause.

The guard turned off the light, hung it on his belt again, and rubbed his mouth as if he was thirsty. Slinging his rifle over his shoulder, he went down the corridor toward the lobby end and out into the connecting hall and out of sight.

"He's gone," Sancho Gomez whispered. He was in the best position to see the lobby door. Elias took the opportunity to get up on his knees and make one more try at picking the lock.

"I think I've got—" he started to say, and then there was a sharp snap. "Damn, it broke."

"Well, fish it out," Caleb whispered to his son.

"I am, I am," Elias whispered back.

"Here he comes," Sancho hissed, and again Elias dropped to the floor, pressing himself close to the wall.

The guard did not look in this time, but went back to his chair. Elias, having done his best, decided he should give up at this point. He crawled across the floor to his bunk. Caleb and

Sancho, heads up to watch, took back their pillows while Elias crawled under his blanket again.

"What are we going to do now?" Thomas Lee whispered in the semidarkness.

"I think I've got an idea," Maggie Blodgett whispered back. "Just sit tight."

Moving in a completely natural fashion, she threw off her blanket and got out of her cot. The guard, noticing the movement, looked up. She went to the door, moving clumsily as if still asleep, and pounded on the glass. The guard, leveling his rifle, got to his feet and came over to the door.

"Bathroom," Maggie shouted. The guard cocked his head as if he hadn't heard. "Bathroom," Maggie said again, mouthing the word exaggeratedly. The guard nodded, took out a key, unlocked the door, and stood well back. He'd gone through this routine a number of times before, and had never had any trouble and didn't expect any now. But his rifle was aimed squarely at Maggie's middle. She gave him no excuse to fire, but stepped away from the door, waited for him to relock it, and then preceded him to the bathroom.

As before, once she was inside with the door locked, the guard stepped away and looked across the corridor into the rebel's prison. Had he wanted, he could have watched her every move inside, as she had watched his not that long ago. But he respected her privacy. After a moment she knocked at the glass, and he let her out and escorted her back to the rest of the rebels. The same sequence of events had happened so many times before there was no reason to suspect anything this time.

"So what did that accomplish?" one of the other women asked.

"I got a piece of the toilet-paper holder," Maggie whispered back.

"That was real sharp," Elias whispered sarcastically. "We can use it to make a pistol and shoot our way out."

"No, stupid," Maggie said. "This thing *is* sharp." They could hear her moving, but could not see what she was doing.

Then she gasped and there was the sound of a piece of metal being thrown into a corner. She got to her feet again, clutching her left arm. Even in the shadows, they could see the blood welling from the self-inflicted wound.

"My God," Julie said, "what have you done?"

"Cut myself on the bunk," Maggie answered, going back to the door.

"But there's nothing sharp on the bunks," Mike protested.

"That's why I got a piece of the toilet-paper holder," Maggie told him, pounding on the glass.

The guard's eyes widened when he saw her upheld arm with the blood streaming off the elbow. He dashed toward the lobby. Mike Donovan and Caleb Taylor immediately rushed over to support Maggie, who obligingly slumped in their arms. They stood within inches of the door.

The guard came back a moment later, carrying a khaki-colored box with a large red cross printed on it. Leveling his rifle at the door, he inserted his key in the lock, turned it, then stepped back. Mike reached out and pushed the door open.

"Back," the guard said, stepping farther back himself. "Just step away from the door."

"She's hurt," Mike said. "My God, she's bleeding to death."

"So fix it," the guard said. Without lowering his rifle, he tossed the first-aid kit in at their feet. Only then did he step forward, both hands on the rifle. "Back," he said again, and the three in the doorway had to comply. The guard shut the door, locked it, and went to sit in his chair. As he sat down, he smiled.

"Damn, that man is good," Caleb said as he and Mike helped Maggie to a chair.

Juliet got the kit and came over to inspect the wound. "Nice to know," she said, "how competent our National Guard is."

Maggie just looked away while Julie applied antiseptic and bandages.

It was three o'clock in the morning. The rebels, in spite of all the rest they'd had during the day, were sleeping. They'd talked over several plans after Maggie's wound had been dressed, but they could come up with no ideas. Darkness, boredom, and a suffocating sense of futility had closed their eyes.

Juliet Parrish lay on her bunk in the middle of the room next to Mike Donovan's, but tossing fitfully. Neither completely asleep nor awake, she dreamed once again that she was fleeing down endless corridors, pursued by a nameless something that had certain obscene ideas about what it wanted to do with her when it caught her.

Under the circumstances, the hand on her shoulder should have made her jump, but it was so gentle, so reassuring, that she just rolled over and opened her eyes. Elizabeth Maxwell stood by her bed, staring down at her.

"Why, Elizabeth," Julie said, "what are you doing here?"

The little girl, far less than a year old but looking as if she were at least nine, didn't answer. But Mike had heard Julie's question, and he sat up, rubbing his eyes.

"Elizabeth," he said, "I thought the guards were taking care of you."

Elizabeth just stared at him. Then she turned and took a few steps toward the door. Mike and Julie remained sitting, and when she realized they weren't following her, Elizabeth stopped to look back at them.

"What's going on?" Elias asked. "Goddamn," he said when he saw Elizabeth. He moved quickly and quietly from his cot to look at the guard in the corridor while the other rebels slowly and confusedly came awake.

"He's asleep," Elias whispered from the window.

"Who?" Sancho Gomez asked.

"The guard, dummy." He turned to Elizabeth. "How did you get in here?"

Without a word, Elizabeth went to the door and put her hand over the lock. Around her outstretched fingers, tiny sparklets of light glittered and winked. Almost soundlessly, the lock clicked and the door swung outward.

By this time all the rebels were awake and alert. Caleb and Sancho joined Elias and Elizabeth at the door.

"You're an amazing child," Elias said while his father and the one-time gardener slipped out into the corridor.

The guard didn't have a chance. Caleb hit him on the side of the head while Sancho kept him from falling and making any noise. They dragged him back inside while the others came out.

Thomas Lee was the first to the hall door at the end of the

corridor. "Looks quiet out here," he whispered back at the rest.

"Elizabeth," Mike said, holding both of her shoulders, "that was wonderful. Now, do you know where our guns are?"

"Pretinama," Elizabeth said, the Visitor word for "peace."

"Yes, Elizabeth," Julie said, *"pretinama.* But first we have to have our guns. Do you understand that?"

Elizabeth turned and went past Lee into the hall that connected their corridor with the central lobby. There were several doors on either side of the hall. She put her hand on one of the knobs and again there were sparklets and glisters, and the door opened.

Mike and Lee rushed up. Inside, on shelves among stacks of linen, were their weapons.

"It looks like the Visitors' guns are here too," Thomas Lee said as he passed the pistols and rifles out to the rebels.

"That's our next stop," Mike said. With Lee beside him, he led the others into the lobby area.

The overhead lights had been turned down but not completely off. There was no one in sight, but the central hall, leading to the back of the building with stairs going up one side to the second floor, was bright and they could hear muted conversation.

Quietly they crossed the lobby to the far hall which led to the other wing. The door at the other end, opening into the corridor, was open, and Mike could see the guard in there, slowly pacing back and forth.

He watched for a moment until he could see the pattern in the guard's movements. Then one more time the guard came toward the hall door, turned, and Mike stepped through immediately behind him. The guard, sensing a presence, turned to find Mike's pistol nearly touching the bridge of his nose. He froze.

Coming round either side, Caleb and Elias grabbed the guard, disarmed him, stuffed his tie into his mouth, and bound his arms with his belt. Meanwhile, Sancho and Juliet, with the others close behind, hurried down to the far end, peering in through each glass wall as they passed.

"Here they are," Sancho said, coming to the twin rooms

that corresponded with the ones they themselves had been held in. "Hey, Mike," he whispered back, "get the key."

But Elizabeth was already there, and for the third time they witnessed the unexplained powers of the half-breed child as her hand, touching the lock, coruscated and sparkled. The door swung open.

It was a confused moment as rebels and fifth columnists greeted each other. But at last Julie asked, "Where's Diana?"

"She's gone," Martin told her. He explained briefly how Diana and Zenia had asked to be put in a separate room.

"Then just before supper," Barbara went on, "three of your people came to visit her. They were just across from us, in this room here, and we could see everything."

"Couldn't hear a word, of course," Ralph said, "but they were civilians, very well dressed, like executives or politicians. They spoke with Diana for over an hour. And then they took her and Zenia away."

"I think she's finally got her lever," Julie said.

"Convertees?" Mike asked rhetorically.

"Or their agents," Julie said.

"She could coordinate an entire counterrevolutionary movement," Martin said grimly.

"I know," Mike responded, "and we've got to stop her. But first, we have to get out of this place."

The soldier who had been guarding the rebels groaned once and rolled over onto his back. He lay still for a long moment, then put his hand to his head. It felt sticky and ached so much that he wanted to throw up. His hand dropped, and he lay still again, then rolled back onto his stomach and forced himself to his knees. Blood dripped, but he didn't see it. His stomach heaved, and he spat bile.

He sat back on his haunches, and slowly the scene around him began to make sense. At first he thought he'd tied one on and had passed out. It had happened before. He'd wakened in a bathroom or an alley and not known where he was. But when he recognized the room where the rebels had been kept, he knew that that was not the explanation.

Still on his knees, he turned toward the door. He remembered then the blow to his head, though he'd been half asleep at the time, and once more he touched the bloody swelling.

His prisoners had escaped. He climbed dazedly to his feet, using the doorjamb for support. The hall beyond was empty, but then it would be. He paused a moment to vomit again and then, feeling slightly better, went down the corridor to the hall and from there to the main lobby.

The other guards were in the back of the building, but he did not go to them. His career was ruined, but maybe he could salvage something. Instead, he went to one of the doors in the connecting hallway and stepped inside.

There was a tiny office, and on the minuscule desk was a phone. He picked it up and dialed a number he knew all too well. After ten rings, somebody finally answered.

"Colonel Fletcher?" he asked.

"Yes, dammit, what is it?"

"This is Private Higgins at the sanitarium. The rebels have escaped, but they're still in the building."

Fully armed, the group of rebels and fifth columnists went cautiously back to the central lobby. Elizabeth immediately started for the front door, but Mike Donovan and Martin paused by the middle hall, from the other end of which they could hear the soft murmur of voices.

This hall led to where the sanitarium staff had had their offices, and which their captors had since adapted to their own temporary uses. There were four off-duty Guardsmen present, getting ready for the next shift. Mike, Martin, Caleb, and Elias stepped into the room, guns leveled. The guards were taken totally by surprise and surrendered without a shot being fired.

The other rebels and Visitors came in and in short order the four Guardsmen were securely bound.

"Where's Diana?" Mike asked the corporal in charge.

"I don't know," the corporal said. "We weren't given that information."

"After Diana and Zenia were put in another room," Martin said, "three civilians came to see her. Who were they?"

"I'm sorry," the corporal said. "All I know is that they had passes signed by Colonel Fletcher. That's all I was concerned about."

"And you just let these men take Diana away on their own authority?" Mike asked incredulously.

"Absolutely not. Colonel Fletcher authorized her removal by phone after the men finished talking with her. I spoke to him myself."

"Who placed the call, the colonel or these men?"

"Mr. Barnabas placed the call. I didn't listen in, but they spoke for several minutes before I was called in to receive the order placing Diana and Zenia into their custody."

"I don't like the sound of that," Caleb Taylor said. "Are you sure it was Fletcher you spoke to?"

"Yes, sir. We used recognition codes."

"But why would Fletcher want Diana taken away?" Juliet Parrish asked.

"I was not given that information," the corporal told her.

"And you have no idea who they were?" Mike insisted.

"No, sir."

"I think they were federal agents," one of the privates said.

"Shut up, Stockwell," the corporal snapped.

"I'm sorry, Tom," Stockwell said. "This whole business is wrong. These people," he nodded at his captors, both human and Visitor, "have no business being locked up in here."

"You follow your orders," the corporal said.

"Not when you know they're wrong. And I'm saying right now, for the record, that I believe keeping Mr. Donovan and Miss Parrish and these others prisoner is wrong."

"You don't know what you're talking about," another private said.

"The hell I don't. Who was it fed us a line of bullshit about the chemicals the Visitors needed? Who was it kept promising us technology and then finding excuses not to pay off? Diana, that's who. And who was it finally found a way to make the Visitors go home? Donovan and Parrish and the other rebels and fifth columnists. But do we treat them like heroes? No, we accuse them of collaboration on the one hand, and of sabotage on the other, and then we lock them up."

"You'd better shut up," the corporal growled.

"You want to get out of that chair and make me?" Stockwell taunted. The corporal, firmly bound, could only glare.

"Why do you think these men were federal agents?" Mike asked the private.

"I was on duty in the corridor when they came to talk with Diana," Stockwell said.

"That's right," Martin said. "He was standing right by their door."

"But the rooms are soundproof," Julie objected.

"But the door wasn't closed tight," Stockwell went on. "I couldn't hear all of what they said, but at one point one of the other men—his name was Stover, I think—said something about Diana's having relative freedom and power if she would share her scientific knowledge with them."

"So who's the collaborator, huh?" Caleb Taylor asked angrily. "We bring Diana in as a prisoner and our own government spirits her away."

"But surely Diana didn't agree to such a deal," Martin said. "She believes in the direct approach. Collaboration is not her style at all."

"Well," Stockwell said. "I don't know whether she agreed or not, but a few minutes later Barnabas asked to use the phone, and then we got the orders to let them take Diana and that other woman away."

"It sounds like collaboration to me," Elias said.

"I wouldn't count on it," a fifth columnist named Annie cautioned. "I've served with Diana for a long time. She's not unlikeable when you don't stand between her and her ambition. I think it's perfectly possible for her to *pretend* to go along with these government agents until she found some kind of handle, some way to gain the upper hand."

"You've got a good point," Martin said. "Collaboration may not be her style, but Diana's smart enough to adapt to changing circumstances, such as being held prisoner here."

"Collaboration with the venal members of your government is not the problem," Barbara said. "Diana will just string them along as she did before. The real threat is what she will do once she gains control of somebody who can wield power."

"And she won't be alone," Mike Donovan agreed. "There are other surviving Visitors already out there, worming their way into positions of authority. All Diana has to do is unify and coordinate their efforts." He turned to Stockwell. "Do you have any idea at all where they might have taken her?" he asked.

"No, I'm sorry," Stockwell said. "I know their car had California plates, but that doesn't mean much. It could have been rented."

"The first thing we've got to do," Julie told the others, "is to reorganize ourselves, find out where Ham and Robert and the rest of the group are."

"You're right," Mike agreed. "We've spent too much time here as it is."

Leaving the Guardsmen bound, the mixed group of rebels and fifth columnists went back to the lobby where Elizabeth was still waiting by the double front doors.

"All right, Elizabeth," Barbara said, picking the child up in her arms, "we can go now."

Mike Donovan and Caleb Taylor found that the front doors were unlocked and swung open easily, but before anybody could go through, spotlights out in the courtyard came on, shining brightly through the doors and the windows on either side.

"Damn," Caleb swore as he pulled the doors closed again. People fell to the floor or ducked behind furniture, expecting a fusillade of shots to follow. Instead, there was the crackle of a bullhorn being switched on.

"This is Captain Broadbent," the amplified voice announced. "We have the place completely surrounded. Throw down your weapons and come out with your hands up."

"Not again!" Elias cried. "We should have gotten out when Elizabeth first wanted us to."

"Then we wouldn't have had any clue as to where Diana might have been taken," Martin said while Barbara carried Elizabeth back out of possible lines of fire.

"A lot of good that's going to do us," Sancho Gomez said, moving so he could see out one of the windows.

"Donovan?" the bullhorn voice roared. "Parrish? Tell your people to surrender. You haven't got a chance."

"He's right, you know," came a voice from behind them. It was the guard they'd thought they'd left unconscious in their prison.

"Well, you're not going to get any satisfaction out of it," Caleb said. He strode swiftly toward the man who, losing his cocky grin, stepped backward. But the guard was not quick enough to avoid the black man's powerful blow. Caleb caught him square in the face, and this time when the guard went down, he didn't even moan.

Mike got up from his crouch, went to the door, and pushed one-half of it open just a crack. Light from the spots outside shone through in a brilliant streak across the floor. Rebels and fifth columnists who were caught in it ducked to one side.

"This is Donovan," Mike yelled through the opening. "You've made a mistake."

"Doesn't seem like it, Mr. Donovan," Broadbent's amplified voice answered.

"Diana is the one you want," Mike yelled, "not us. Three men came yesterday afternoon and took her away. She could be free by now, and she can control anybody who has undergone the Visitors' conversion process."

"You're not making much sense," Broadbent called back.

"It's like brainwashing," Mike explained. "Anybody who spent time on the Visitors' ships could have been subjected to it. And Diana can control these people directly with her mind. She's got to be stopped before she—"

"That's as may be," Braodbent said, "but I've got my orders. Colonel Fletcher was very specific. You're to be taken into custody—again—to face charges of collaboration with the enemy and sabotage of the Visitors' bases. We'll worry about Diana later."

"Man, that guy must be stupid," Sancho said. "Can't he see he's contradicting himself?"

"Maybe he can," Martin said, "but his orders seem simple enough."

"Donovan?" Broadbent called. "I'll give you one minute, and then we'll open fire."

"We've got a child in here," Mike called back.

"That's your worry," Broadbent answered.

"Do we fight?" Maggie Blodgett asked uncertainly.

"I think we have to," Juliet said. "If we're taken prisoner again, we may not have Elizabeth to unlock our doors for us."

"There's got to be some other way," Thomas Lee said. "I don't want to shoot at my own people."

"Now you know how it felt for us," Annie told him, "when we fifth columnists had to shoot at *our* own people."

"Annie's right," Julie said. "If you believe in what we stand for, what we're trying to do, you have to accept the consequences."

"That doesn't mean I have to like it," Lee insisted.

"No," Martin said, "it doesn't. Do you want to go out there and surrender?"

"I want to go home," Lee answered simply.

"So do I," Martin snapped. "But it doesn't look like I'm going to get there, and there might not be a home for me even if I was able to go."

"I think we'd better get ready," Mike said. "Our time's almost up."

"Is there a back door?" Elias Taylor asked suddenly. Nobody knew. "Willie, come with me." The two went off to find out how badly they were exposed from the rear.

"Open fire!" Broadbent shouted, and the shooting started.

A few bullets whizzed through the slightly open door, but the reinforced windows, though they crazed and spalled, did not shatter under the small arms fire. The walls were solid, and nobody inside was in any real danger as long as they kept out of the area in front of the door. But they had no place they could shoot from either. Mike and Sancho, keeping their heads down and firing blindly, shot out into the courtyard. There was no room for anybody else to join them.

After a moment the firing from outside ceased. The rebels could tell, from the sounds of moaning and occasional curses and cries of pain, that their shots had been more effective than those of the Guardsmen.

"They're planning something," Caleb Taylor said, coming forward to see if he could find a vantage point.

"Hey," Elias called from the back hall, "there's no back door at all. The windows are holding up, so that front door is the only way in or out of this place."

"Get out of the line of fire," Caleb called to his son. Elias realized only at that instant that he was standing in the streak of light from the open door. He dove to one side just as a burst of machine-gun fire stitched the wall behind where he'd been standing. Some of the shots must have gone down the hall behind him, because the rebels could hear one of the Guardsmen they'd left tied up back there crying out in pain.

"They're rushing from the sides," Mike yelled. He was lying well to one side and could see four or five Guardsmen running toward the door almost against the wall. He fired, saw one fall, and then the door was ripped open by other Guardsmen coming up from the other side. Caleb and Martin fired frantically at this second assault while Mike rolled back out of sight.

But now the troops outside had a larger target. Bullets came through in a deadly hail. The fifth columnist named Lawrence and two of the rebels were not able to find cover in time. Their one-time guard, who was now lying in the beams of the spotlight, was chewed apart by the "friendly" fire.

Still, the open door gave those inside more opportunities to fire as well. And the Visitor weapons were highly effective against two parked vehicles which exploded. The Visitor weapons also set off the amunition in several guns.

At a shouted command from Captain Broadbent, the firing outside stopped for a second time.

"This is your last chance," Broadbent said, once more using the bullhorn. "Throw down your weapons and come out with your hands up."

Mike leaned around the base of the door and fired once. There was a squawk from the bullhorn, which went silent. Then the Guardsmen outside opened fire again.

The rebels weren't able to offer much return fire. They were too busy keeping out of the broad fan of bullets coming through the door and now coming through the windows too, which, despite their strength, could not resist so determined an onslaught or so many hits. All the rebels could do was fire back often enough to discourage any further attempts to rush the door.

From where she crouched with Mike, behind a desk that

would soon not offer any significant protection, Julie could see
the sky beginning to grow bright beyond one of the windows.

"This may be our last morning," she said. In the face of
inevitable defeat, she didn't want to fight anymore.

"We're not licked yet," Mike told her, trying to be
reassuring. But he too did no have much hope.

"It's ironic," Julie said, her voice barely audible above the
noise of the gunfire. "Here we are, just a few people who
successfully threw off an invasion by a force of thousánds of
aliens with superior technology, and now we're about to be
killed by just a few of our own soldiers."

"If it was only us," Mike said, "I'd give up and let them do
what they could. But those soldiers out there are playing right
into Diana's hands."

"Maybe we *should* give up," Julie said. "Dead, we can do
nothing at all. If we surrender, at least we'll be alive and might
be able to do something later."

"I've been thinking about it," Mike admitted when suddenly there was a tremendous explosion from outside the wall
surrounding the sanitarium.

"They're shelling us," Thomas Lee yelled. There was even
more gunfire now and more explosions.

"No," Mike said. "Listen."

"To what?" Julie cried.

"Listen," Mike yelled to the others. "Those're *Visitors*
weapons out there."

"Diana?" Julie asked.

"No," Mike said. "The Fixer!"

The shooting intensified, but less of it was being directed at
the sanitarium now. Inside, the rebels and fifth columnists took
heart and tried to make their own fire more effective.

And then suddenly it broke. The Guardsmen outside started
to retreat, climbing into their trucks and driving off, leaving
their heavier weapons behind. From the hills across the road
which were just visible above the top of the wall, Mike could
see the beams of Visitor weapons as the other group of rebels
closed in.

"Their backside was wide open," Elias yelled. "They didn't
stand a chance!"

"Let's finish this off right now," Caleb said, and with William beside him, he made a rush for the door.

There were no soldiers left in the courtyard, at least none living. The gates in the wall had been torn down. Caleb and William, now followed by most of the others, ran out and fired into the backs of the retreating soldiers. In a few moments it was all over.

The silence was a blessed relief. Ham Tyler, walking with his usual nonchalance, came down from his place on the hill across the road. There were forty or fifty men and women with him. They all looked hard-bitten and wary. Over to one side, Chris Faber signaled to other rebels out of sight.

Mike and Julie walked out to meet the Fixer in the middle of the road while their companions, human and Visitor, cheered the rescuing forces.

"Looks like I got here just in time," Ham said calmly.

"Ten minutes sooner would have been better," Mike said, then turned to see a dozen or more motorcycles roar up. The bikes were chopped, sported Nazi symbols and skulls, and were driven by men whose meanness made Ham look like a kindly uncle. The choppers screeched to a halt just feet from the three, and their leader, a particularly ugly man with a face scarred by fire, casually stepped off his bike, kicked the stand down, and came over to join them.

"That was fun," he said with an incongruously boyish grin.

"I'm glad you enjoyed it," Ham said. To Mike and Julie, he said, "If you were wondering why nobody came in from the back or sides, it was because Gorf and his club here were protecting your flanks."

"They didn't pay any attention to us," Gorf said, "until it was too late. I didn't even have to use my gun." He patted the machine pistol strapped to his thigh. "Just ran them down." Mike looked over at Gorf's chopper and saw that the heavy front fender was dented and bloody.

"You sure can come up with some surprises," he said to Ham. Around them the Fixer's forces were gathering. Those among them who Mike knew greeted the rebels and fifth columnists whom they'd rescued with unfeigned enthusiasm.

"That was Chris's idea," Ham said. "He used to ride with this club a few years back."

"You'd better get your asses in gear," Gorf said. "Those soldiers haven't gone that far away, and in a straight-on fight I think they could take us."

"All right," Ham shouted, turning to address the people milling around. "Let's get a move on." Trucks drove up, and the rebels started getting in.

"Where are we going?" Mike asked.

"We've got a new place," Ham said, "an abandoned mine up in the hills south of L.A." He stepped back to let Barbara, still carrying Elizabeth, go past to one of the trucks. "Robin's there now," he said, "along with Robert and the others. We should pull ourselves together. We've still got a lot of work to do."

"You'd better believe it," Julie said. "Diana has escaped." Quickly she explained what had happened.

"It gets dirtier all the time," Ham said.

"That's the way we like it," Gorf said. "You got any more parties like this in mind, you just let me know."

"I'll do that," Ham told him. The gang leader nodded, then went back to his chopper and with the rest of his club following, drove off.

"All right," Ham yelled again, even as the first of the trucks started off. "Let's get this show on the road."

The trucks, cars, and vans pulled into the open space in front of the main mine building high in the hills south and east of Los Angeles. Thanks to the Visitor communicators, which Grace Delaney and Barry Stine had succeeded in figuring out, Robert Maxwell and the others there had been able to stay in communication with Ham Tyler, and knew beforehand of their friends' approach.

The reunion was joyful. Robin Maxwell insisted on coming out to meet the rebels with her father, and when she saw Elizabeth, there was no holding her. The half-breed child, who had always been rather cool to her mother, seemed genuinely pleased to see her this time.

"She's a very special person," Mike Donovan told Robin and Robert. "It's Elizabeth who disarmed the doomsday bomb before it could go off."

"But how could she possibly do that?" Robin asked, holding her daughter tight.

"We don't really know," Juliet Parrish said. "She just put her hands on the controls, and then it was like she was lit up all over with tiny Christmas tree lights. And after a moment, the bomb just shut off."

"Barbara and I had tried to override the program with a special computer," Mike said, "but nothing we did worked. If it hadn't been for Elizabeth, the whole world would have been destroyed."

"Oh, Elizabeth," Robin said, hugging the child, "I think you're wonderful."

"She works miracles on all levels," Caleb Taylor told her. "She doesn't need just any old doomsday bomb, she can also open prison doors." He told the young mother about the half-breed girl's role in their escape from the sanitarium.

Robin, as she listened to the story, looked at her child in amazement. "Where did she get such powers?" she asked.

"We don't know," Barbara said. "There's nothing like her abilities among our people, though we, as you, have dreamed and speculated about such things for ages."

"It's something we'll have to explore later," Mike said. "We don't need to worry about it now. But we're awfully glad she was with us when she was needed."

"You're not going to experiment on her," Robin asked apprehensively.

"No," her father reassured her, patting her shoulder, "we're not going to do that. But where's Diana?"

"She's escaped," Julie said, "again."

"She's somewhere on Earth," Mike expanded, "in the hands of government officials who offered her freedom in exchange for her knowledge."

"You can't be serious," Robert exclaimed.

"I am, but it's more complicated than that. Right now we have to plan what to do next. You'll hear the whole story when I explain it to everybody else."

"Well, let's get on with it, then," Robert said.

Chapter 10

For the first time since the final invasion on the Los Angeles Mother Ship, all the rebels were together again. Someone had even found out where Arthur Dupres, Mike's stepfather, had taken Sean, and had brought both of them up to the mine.

Mike went to see them in the small room they were sharing. Sean was still rather subdued and withdrawn, and though he tried to pretend to be happy to see his father, the confusion induced by his conversion made his enthusiasm anything but convincing.

"You'll have to give him time," Arthur said a little later when he was alone with his stepson. "He doesn't really comprehend yet what's happened to him."

"If Julie could pull through it," Mike said, "then I guess Sean can too. I felt like a heel, tricking the boy that way so he would give Steven and Mother false information. Sean's always trusted me before."

"He will again. You'll just have to be patient."

"More likely what's going to happen is that I'll be too busy to be *im*patient. But speaking of Mother, do you know how she is?"

Arthur's face grew pained and he turned away. "She's dead, Mike."

Mike stood for a long moment. He had stopped liking his mother long ago, but he still loved her.

"How did it happen?" he asked at last.

"Steven shot her. I don't know the details, but I do know that Ham Tyler made a special point of personally seeing that Steven died. Poured a whole packet of toxin down his throat."

"Ham may have an odd sense of right and wrong," Mike said softly, "but in this case, I think I agree with him."

The rebel force was larger than ever, what with the fifth columnists and the people from other groups which the Fixer had called on for help. Altogether, over seventy-five people gathered in the mine's dining hall to hold a council of war.

Juliet Parrish stood at the head table, looking out over the crowd. She'd tried to get Mike or Ham or even Martin to take over leadership of the group, but they'd all refused, saying she was the person the rebels believed in, she was the one who should make the decisions.

"Attention, everybody," Julie said. "We've got a lot of things to discuss. First, what happened to the suspended people we brought down to the processing plant?"

"Those who were revived were set free," Claire Bryant said. "The others are still in their coffins, as far as we know. The people who took over the plant were no more successful than we were in figuring out how the equipment worked."

"How long before they start dying," Julie asked.

"How long has it been?" Phyllis, the fifth columnist, asked. Somebody told her. "They should be all right for a couple more days," Phyllis said. "Then they'll start dying."

"Have any more suspendees been brought down?" Julie queried.

"No," Grace Delaney said. "I don't understand it. No attempt was made to learn how to use the shuttles. All three are still at the plant."

"So then," Mike said, "nobody has gone up to the Mother Ship since we came down."

"That's right," Grace told him. "Like I said, it makes no sense."

"It does," Julie said, "if you understand that the people

who are giving orders have all been converted. Without supervision, they've lost almost all initiative. Worse, they can't choose between doing what's best for Earth or what's best for the Visitors."

"That seems consistant with what we've been hearing on the news," Paul Overbloom said. "Nobody can make up their minds. Our politicians keep contradicting themselves and each other."

"Exactly," Juliet said. "Now what's the chance of our getting one of these shuttles?"

"They're all guarded," Fred Linker said, "but I think we could take one if we wanted to badly enough."

"We may," Julie told him. "Any word from our allies on the Mother Ship?"

"We've been trying to establish communications," Barry Stine said, "but we've had little success. Every time we get a clear signal, somebody overrides it."

"It's got to be the turncoats," Elias offered. He explained briefly to those who had not been in the Mother Ship about the traitors among the fifth columnists. "At least," he concluded, "if what you're telling us is any indication, they haven't yet taken over the ship."

"I don't think so," Barry said. "But I don't think anybody up there is going to be of any help to us."

"If the turncoats did take over," Julie asked, turning to Martin, "what's the worst they could do?"

"Use the ship's weapons to destroy a large part of Los Angeles," Martin answered. "I don't think that's a real possibility, though. What's more likely is that somebody who doesn't know what he's doing will try to take the ship away again. If that were to happen, considering the repairs that still need to be done, then there's a strong possibility that the gravity generators would give out and the ship would just fall on Los Angeles."

"That would flatten most of the city," someone said.

"Worse than that," Martin corrected, "the power generators would all discharge at once. It wouldn't blow the world apart, but it would sure turn all of southern California into a mighty big lake."

"It seems as if the thing to do," Julie said, "is to go back up to the Mother Ship and disarm the turncoats."

"I think you're right," Robert Maxwell agreed. "And there are still nearly ten thousand suspended human beings up there."

"Not to mention those of our people whom we've tested and know we can trust," the fifth columnist, Ralph, said.

"Sounds good," Ham said sarcastically. "And then when we have all our friends down here, then what will we do? Let the police arrest them? Let the National Guard put them in sanitariums? Let some converted general bring out the whole army?"

"But we're going to be bringing down *humans*," Maggie said. "Helpless victims. And as far as I know, the few Visitors here are the only people who know how to remove them from suspended animation and bring them back to life. Could anybody stop us from doing that?"

"They did before," the Visitor named George said. "Your Colonel Fletcher didn't even let us finish with the ones we brought on the first trip."

"He didn't know what he was doing," Sancho Gomez said. "If we could let them know what we were intending to do beforehand, they might at least let us bring these people out of suspended animation."

"That's a point," Julie said. "At least it will buy us some time."

"It may take more time than they're willing to allow," Martin objected. "Even if our technicians train you sufficiently so you can help with the unprocessing, it will be a slow business. Your politicians and generals might not have that much patience."

"This is really bizarre," Elias Taylor said, "using our own people as hostages against our own government."

"It is that," Mike Donovan agreed, "but if it will work, we'll have to do it. We need all the time we can get so we can learn about how to deconvert those politicians and generals and get them back on our side."

"And that's our real problem," Juliet said. "Right now we don't know how many Visitor survivors have been able to make contact with convertees and gain control of them. We don't even know how many convertees there are. And nothing we do will be of any lasting benefit if the government remains in the hands of people whose minds are confused at best, and controlled by our enemies at worst."

"We're talking about several different and very distinct things here," Ham Tyler said. "Those people who have been converted are not going to just come right out and tell us so. We're going to have to do some pretty heavy undercover work to learn all the names."

"Well," Mike said, "that's your job."

"No, it's not," Ham said. "I'm not in that kind of intelligence."

"But you know people who are."

"Ye-e-s."

"Okay, then you're it. You're better qualified than any of the rest of us. You know people."

"Ye-e-s," Ham said again. He glared around the room. "It's going to take some time," he said, "and it won't do any good if Diana is still out there pulling her tricks. With the contacts she's made, she'll be able to undermine all our plans."

"And that's the crux of the situation," Mike agreed. "Whoever it was that got Colonel Fletcher to release her into their custody, they're not pikers. She's gotten into the real power structure here. Either they'll be strong enough to manipulate her to their ends or, which is more likely, she will gain control of them."

"There's still the toxin to consider," Barbara said. "Some of our people have been feeling slightly unwell lately, all with the same symptoms—difficulty in breathing, racing pulse. I haven't felt it myself, and I was one of the first to get the antitoxin, of which we're going to need a lot more very soon. Maybe if we just wait, Diana's dose will wear off, and the problem will take care of itself."

"We can't take the chance," Julie said. "If we, with our limited resources and equipment, could make the antitoxin, surely any well-equipped hospital could do the same. And besides, some of you have a natural immunity, and—" She had to pause while a number of the fifth columnists absorbed this news. "I'll tell you about that later. There are also, respirators. Not convenient, but effective if used properly. And there's no guarantee that Diana couldn't come up with the antitoxin herself. After all, she's your most intelligent and well-trained scientist—and a life scientist at that."

"No matter how we look at it," Elias said, "it all comes back to the same thing. Diana is the key to this whole business."

"We've had her in our hands before," Caleb Taylor said gently, "and it didn't do us any good."

"I know, Pop, but without her we've got nothing because she can always screw up anything we can do. Especially now. I don't know who those guys were who took her away yesterday, but you can bet your bottom that whoever they were, they offered her a position of power. Now *we've* got to find ourselves a similar position of power."

"There's another side to this," Mike Donovan said. "Diana may not have power, but she can influence people. We have to counter that. And the only way to do that, as far as I can see, is to inform people of the danger, spread the news as far and as loudly as we can."

"I think you're right," Julie said. "After all, more than ninety-five percent of the people out there don't know what's going on, have never known since the Visitors took over our news services."

"That's it," Mike said. "And how did they do that?"

"They overrode our TV and radio signals," Grace Delaney said. "They broadcast their version of everything, even when national and local stations didn't cooperate."

"That's right," Mike said. "And they did that from up on their ship. Which also, so I'm told, has pretty powerful military weapons as well."

"So we go back up there one more time," Maggie Blodgett said.

"Exactly."

"Not me," Ham protested. "There are too many things for me to do down here. You said so yourself."

"Oh, no," Mike told him. "This time, *everybody* goes up. You, me, Robin, Elizabeth, the children, everybody."

"But why?" Robin asked.

"Because that's the one place where nobody on Earth can

touch us. And that's the one place from which we can control the communications of this country, if not of the whole world."

"But there are turncoats up there," William protested.

"We'll take care of them," Mike said. "But we've got to get up there first."

"And there are three of the largest shuttles just waiting for us at the suspension plant," Caleb said.

Overhead lights shone down on the paved area behind the plant where so many people had been put into suspended animation. The three shuttles stood fully illuminated. They looked as though they hadn't been moved. Three or four National Guardsmen, their rifles hanging from their shoulders, patrolled the area with a casual, bored manner.

From their hiding places in the tire dump, the rebels watched the area. Everybody was here now, even the children.

"I don't like it," Ham Tyler said to Mike, Julie, Elias, and Martin. "It's just too quiet. With all the action that's gone on here during the last few days, you'd think they'd have more men on guard."

"Whoever is giving the orders has probably been converted," Juliet Parrish said.

"Or else they suspect we're coming," Elias Taylor offered, "and have set a trap for us."

"I suppose that's possible," Mike Donovan said, "but they can't know how many of us there are. We're going to have to try for it anyway."

"Might as well get it over with," Ham agreed. He looked over at another stack of tractor tires where Chris Faber was conferring with several rebels. After a moment Chris looked back at his colleague and nodded. The other rebels moved off.

"That's it," the Fixer said. He passed the silent message on to other rebels who could see his signal and who in turn sent it on to still others. People started moving, spreading out as they neared the fence. Ham kept his eye on Chris, who had remained at his post, and after what seemed like an awfully long time Chris, who had been watching someone else out of sight, gave Ham another hand sign.

"All right," Ham said. He drew and cocked his weapon,

Martin did the same. Mike and Julie and Elias put down their own weapons, stood up from their hiding place, and with no attempt at concealment walked toward the gate in the fence.

The soldiers on guard didn't see them until they had swung the gate open. The Guardsmen didn't seem at all concerned, though they unslung their rifles and held them at ready.

Mike walked up to the nearest guard. "We've come to ask about the suspended people who were brought here recently," he said. "Some of them may be friends of ours. Do you know if any more have been revived?"

"They're all still there," the guard said, "still in those plastic coffins." The other three soldiers came closer, keeping their eyes on the three rebels.

"I don't think they can stay in that condition indefinitely," Julie told him. "Have you been able to bring any more back from the ship?"

"They can't figure out how to open the hatches," one of the other guards said. He seemed calm enough, but he kept his gun at the ready.

"You should get a couple of Caltech students," Elias suggested. "They can break into anything."

"You know any?" the first guard started to say, and then the rebels Chris had dispatched appeared behind them.

"Just lay them down easy," Mike said. The guards knelt to put their rifles on the pavement.

"Too easy," Elias said as the other rebels used the soldiers' belts to tie them up. Other people now moved across the field, quickly but quietly barricading the plant door. Phyllis, Joanna, and Ralph hurried from their hiding places to the shuttle hatches and triggered the codes that opened them.

"Much too easy," Ham repeated, coming up from behind. "Unless opening those shuttles was exactly what they wanted us to do." The entire rebel force was now hurrying across the pavement toward the three shuttles.

"It's not going to help them much," Caleb Taylor told him, brandishing a large pair of wire cutters. "Their phone line's gone on the blink, and their doors are jammed." He shook his head in mock dismay.

The rebels were loading quickly. The children were taken on

early, leaving only adults exposed in case there should be trouble.

"Do we need all three of those things?" Ham asked.

"No sense leaving one for our enemies," Julie told him. Just then the lights started coming on in the plant, and seconds later there were shouts.

"All right," Ham shouted, walking deliberately across the area, herding the last of the rebels before him. "Let's get moving."

The soldiers inside the plant had discovered that they were effectively locked in, and were now trying to smash their way out. But Ham's plan had been too thorough and had been carried off to perfection. The soldiers were effectively trapped.

As soon as the full import of this came to them, the soldiers started shooting from every available window. The last of the rebels, caught outside the shuttles, returned the fire, but the shuttle hatches were facing the building, and Mike, Julie, Ham, and the rest who had not yet boarded were unable to enter them now. They could only crouch behind the shuttles, firing back at the soldiers. Other rebels shot from safe positions just inside the shuttle hatches.

"I *knew* it was too damn easy," Ham shouted. "They won't stay penned up in there long, and then they'll have the shuttles, just like they planned."

"I wouldn't be too sure of that," Mike said as the shuttle nearest the building's loading docks suddenly lifted up a few inches and started swinging around. He couldn't tell who was at the controls, but he suspected it was Martin. The nose of the shuttle slowly turned toward the double doors, and then the craft's heavy weapons fired. The shots, showing Martin's marksmanship, were aimed perfectly, fusing the doors shut while driving the soldiers behind them to deeper cover.

Meanwhile the other two shuttles had also lifted a few inches and turned 180 degrees, so that the hatches were now facing away from the plant. While elevated, the rebels on the ground were exposed to enemy fire, but the first shuttle placed its shots strategically, spoiling the soldiers' aim.

When this subtle maneuver was completed, the last of the rebels were at last able to climb aboard. The shuttle hatches were just closing on them as one set of garage doors finally gave way, spilling fully armed soldiers into the area. The soldiers fired at the shuttles as they started their ascent, and sirens started belatedly going off. From somewhere beyond the front of the building came the sound of racing engines as more troops were finally mobilized. But by the time the soldiers got there, the shuttles were just specks in the black night sky.

Chapter 11

The shuttles received no challenge as they approached the underbelly of the Mother Ship. Martin tried to raise the flight controller, but there was no response.

"How do we get inside?" Julie asked.

"I can trigger an emergency override from here," Martin said, opening a safety cover on the control panel to reveal a red button inside. He pushed it, and the docking-bay doors slid open.

The three shuttles drifted in and settled down on the deck. There was nobody in sight. The sound of the three hatches coming open echoed hollowly in the cavernous space.

"I hope there's somebody left alive," Martin said.

"We never did find out how many turncoats there were," Caleb said. "You don't suppose they've taken over the ship?"

"They could have," Barbara said, panting. Caleb reached out a hand to steady her.

"What's the matter?" he asked her.

"I've not been feeling too well the last half hour—short of breath, pains in my chest."

"It sounds like your antitoxin is wearing off," Julie said, "and you've been exposed for a long time down on Earth. We're going to have to get a new supply made up as soon as possible. I wish we hadn't lost what we'd made at the mine." The others who had been on the shuttle were now out on the deck, so she and her friends in the cockpit followed them out now.

Sancho Gomez and William, who'd come up in one of the other shuttles and had been among the first to disembark, were moving along the elevated catwalk toward the flight controller's office, high above the docking-bay floor.

"There's no one inside," Sancho called down to the others.

"Can you operate the communicator in there?" Mike Donovan yelled back.

"I can," William said, and stepped into the glass-fronted booth. They could see him punching buttons, then talking into the microphone.

"It's all right," he said as he came back out onto the catwalk. "Peter and Aaron are in the command center. They've got the ship under control, but there are still some armed turncoats loose, and people are beginning to get sick."

"We've got to make that antitoxin fast," Julie said. She and Barbara went over to the shuttle that had carried her equipment while Mike and Martin and the others who knew their way started leading the newcomers toward the command center.

Grace Delaney and Fred Linker were handing boxes out to Paul Overbloom and Claire Bryant.

"Let those go till later," Julie told them. "We need the ones marked with the green circle right now."

"They're the next ones in the stack," Grace said.

"Fine, get them all and come with me. We've got to work fast or a lot of the fifth columnists will die."

"But there's no toxin in here now," Barbara said. "At least there shouldn't be."

"Perhaps not," Julie said, "but everybody who was down on Earth was exposed to it and so may be carrying some in their systems. You're probably breathing it out of your lungs right now. Those of your people who were never exposed at all will probably be all right for a little while, but everybody else is going to need a new dose."

At last everybody except Juliet Parrish and her crew was moving toward the command center. Instead, she and those who would be making the antitoxin went to the labs. In the absolute silence of the ship, they were taken by surprise by a turncoat who, waiting on the other side of a corner, fired on them. Phyllis was hit in the shoulder and dropped her box, and the others, encumbered by their own loads, were not able to return fire before the turncoat turned and fled.

"Don't let him get away," Juliet commanded, putting down her box and drawing her gun. While someone attended to Phyllis, she and the others raced after the Visitor, who had turned into a long corridor. He was a hundred yards ahead, but the concentrated fire of seven guns brought him down.

Returning to where Phyllis was getting painfully to her feet, they recovered their supplies and went on to the labs.

Meanwhile, Mike Donovan and the main rebel force found Peter and Aaron in the command center with half a dozen other visitors. None of them looked well.

"Thank God you're back," Peter said. "There was no way we could have gone down to get you, and now we're all coming down sick with something."

"It's the effect of the toxin," Mike explained. "Those who were exposed before still have some in their systems, and the antitoxin is wearing off. Julie's making up a new batch right now," he reassured them. "Are you all right otherwise?"

"We are now," Peter said. "We weren't sure you were ever going to come back and were beginning to give up hope. We've had the tables turned on us. I think there are only a dozen or so turncoats, but they're playing guerrilla against us just like we did when we were in the minority. A couple of people have been hurt, but nobody killed. What took you so long?"

Between them, Mike and Martin and Ham Tyler told about the betrayal, imprisonment, and rescue, concluding with the news that Diana had escaped yet again, and this time seemed to have some human friends.

"She'll have to wait her turn," Aaron said. "Those turncoats will have to be attended to first. None of us are very good leaders. I'm sure you wouldn't have let the turncoats stay free for so long, but with you back, we should be able to make the ship really secure."

"Most of those who we confined to quarters," Peter went on, "are still there. We just haven't been able to test them."

"We'll get to that when we have time," Martin said, holding his hand to his chest as if he was having some difficulty breathing. "Right now we need more antitoxin."

Juliet Parrish came through with the antitoxin before any of the Visitors became seriously ill. Fortunately, not all of those who had been exposed suffered ill effects, and were able to renew the business of administering truth serum to the rest of the crew. Those who passed the truth test were given their freedom, and those who failed were consolidated in secure quarters. It looked as if about one in four were going to prove sympathetic to the human cause. That made for a mighty thin crew, but enough to keep the ship operating in its stationary position over Los Angeles.

Even before those who had been taken sick had time to recover, Mike, Julie, Martin, Barbara, Grace, Peter, Fred, and Annie started planning their next step. Their primary concern, aside from Diana's whereabouts, was to inform the public of the facts concerning the conversion process. The ship's communications center was capable of interrupting and over-riding television and radio broadcasting, even to the extent of controlling the phone lines linking studios to transmitting towers. Julie had taken advantage of this fact when she had announced the return of the Mother Ship so recently.

This time they would have to do a better job, both in the preparation of the message and in timing its broadcast. With the assistance of several proven communications technicians, the eight rebels and fifth columnists set to work making a videotape that they would be able to play over and over again, at least once an hour during the day and night. Using the Visitors' translating equipment, they prepared versions in every major language, even though with only one ship they could not directly influence the broadcasts in countries that were out of line of the transmission. They could, however, put the message through regular communications satellites, and hope that other broadcasters around the world would play it voluntarily.

Caught between the need to get the message on the air as soon as possible and the need to take the time to do it right, they had to compromise. Twenty-four hours after returning to the Mother Ship, the tape, though not perfect, was done.

All over the United States, Canada, and Mexico, TV programs were interrupted. Even radio stations carried the message. Those who saw it on TV saw four humans and four Visitors, sitting or standing in a huge room with incomprehensible instruments, devices, and controls humming and blinking all around them. It was the command center, and in the background other rebels and Visitors went about their business.

"People of the United States," Julie said, "and of the world, my name is Juliet Parrish. A short while ago I spoke to you announcing our return to Earth in the great Los Angeles Mother Ship. We are speaking to you from there now. Our forces, the very same who devised and executed the plan that drove the Visitors from your skies, are in complete control of this ship, its resources, its technology.

"Those Visitors you see with us have demonstrated a loyalty higher than that to any one person or government or race, or even world. They are loyal to all of humanity, whether mammalian or reptilian. Between us, we can restore order to our now confused planet, and perhaps, in time, to their planet as well.

"There are some Visitors among you, left behind when the rest of their fleet departed in such haste. We beg that you treat these survivors both with caution and with respect. Some will be your enemies, some your friends, and we have the means of determining which is which. We beg that you neither give these Visitors your trust until proven, nor kill them out of hand. They should all be taken into custody, given an antitoxin treatment which a number of laboratories and hospitals can provide, and kept safe until they can be tested.

"The Visitors among you can be easily identified because of their voices. But there are others, perhaps less trustworthy though many of them may be innocent, who cannot be so easily marked. I'm speaking of any person who, for whatever reason, ever spent any time aboard a Visitor ship during the last year."

Mike took over at this point and explained about the process of conversion. Martin and Barbara helped by describing the process and what it was supposed to do to people. Julie told of her own experience, and Mike told how it had affected his son, Sean. He went on to describe the extent of the danger, citing their own arrest as evidence of the untrustworthiness of any government official, any person in power who had been converted, whether they were being controlled by a Visitor or not.

They concluded with a plea.

"Those of you," Julie said, "who suspect you may have been converted, whether you remember it happening to you or not, can fight back. With the help of your families and friends, you can discover whether or not you have ever been under Visitor control. Accepting that, and knowing how it has affected you, is the first and biggest step.

"I can testify from my own experience that conversion is not absolute, not irreversible. In time, we will have perfected a method of returning all convertees to normal. In the meantime, listen to your friends. Listen to your families. Try to resist the brainwashing that has been done to you. And if you cannot resist, let someone else temporarily assume your responsibilities. Except for our friends here, the Visitors have gone. But this war is not won yet."

During the next twelve hours, while Mike Donovan and Juliet Parrish and the others who had participated in preparing the message slept, the business of testing the Visitor crew members continued. At the same time, a new organization of those found trustworthy was developed to make the best use of the radically reduced crew. Monitors were set up to receive the major network programming in order to learn how the message had gone over and to plan out revisions accordingly, should that be necessary.

Elsewhere, the humans held in suspended animation were attended to preparatory to returning them to the Los Angeles plant for unprocessing. Though there was equipment aboard the ship that could do that, the rate of revival was very low. It had never been intended to bring the grim cargo back to life on board.

Still, two humans an hour were brought back to life. Most of these people could be of little help to the rebel forces, being just plain citizens from San Pedro and elsewhere, not soldiers or technicians or doctors. The extra human population was something of a burden, since the ship was not equipped to provide much in the way of human food. Still, it was thought better to bring as many out of suspension as possible in order to shorten the process once they were sure they could return to the Earth plant.

Aaron, Arnold, Caleb Taylor, and Robert Maxwell were in charge in the command center when William came in, in a state of excitement.

"I think there are some Visitors alive in one of the compartments where the bodies are being kept," he said. "Maybe in more than one. I didn't believe it at first when people reported sounds coming from inside, but I went to one and I could hear it too, like someone knocking on the door."

"How can there be survivors?" Arnold, the conversion technician, asked.

"It must be that natural immunity Julie mentioned," Aaron said.

"It has to be that," Robert agreed. "Apparently, instead of just dying, they go catatonic for a period of time of from two to four days, and then recover. It's happened on Earth."

"I thought all those survivors had respirators," Arnold said, "or else were in uncontaminated areas."

"Most of them were, but not all."

"We can't just leave them in those compartments with all those dead bodies," William said.

"What a nightmare," Caleb Taylor agreed. "Waking up sick to death in a pile of rotting corpses and probably starving too."

"But we can't just let them out," Aaron objected. "They're heavily contaminated with the toxin, and the greater the concentration, the shorter the effective period of the anti-toxin."

"We can take a portable air lock with us," Arnold suggested. "Just a bag we can seal around the door, with us inside, before we open it. And then, if anybody's alive inside, we can seal them up in suspension coffins while we take them somewhere to be decontaminated."

"But then *we'll* be contaminated," Caleb objected.

"We'll carry an air tank and filter. When we're ready to

leave, we'll flush out the air lock into the filter and dump that off the ship."

"There may be some risk," Aaron went on, "but we shouldn't let too much of the toxin into the ship. I find the idea of leaving anybody alive in one of those mausoleums intolerable. Let's do it."

The first mortuary compartment that Caleb, Arnold, Aaron, Robert, and William visited had no survivors. As a last-minute idea, Aaron had suggested that they all wear respirators, and that proved to be a good idea, since the stench of the decaying bodies would otherwise have overwhelmed them.

In the second compartment, they found a woman who had died only recently. In the third compartment, however, they found three who were still alive—two women and a man. They sealed these three up in suspension coffins and after preliminary decontamination in their portable air lock, left them in the corridor to be picked up by a follow-up crew.

When they entered the fourth compartment, they thought at first that none were alive. But even as they were turning to leave, one of the bodies, that of a large captain wearing the disguise of a black man, turned over and fired. Aaron fell with a cry.

Caleb strode into the mass of putrefaction and grabbed the gun out of the captain's hand. The survivor was too weak to resist.

"Aaron's dead," Arnold reported, crouching down to examine his friend.

"Maybe we should just leave this guy here," Caleb said, pointing the gun at the black captain's head.

"No," Robert objected. "I want this man alive. This is the guy who promised he'd let me get my family away from the mountain camp if I'd tell him where it was." He came over and stood beside Caleb, looking down at Jake. "Your word as a father," he said. "My wife died because of your treachery. I want to see you face whatever punishment they decide is appropriate." He stepped back and helped William wrestle in a suspension coffin.

"Where's Diana?" Jake asked, his voice a weak rasp.

"Not where you're ever going to find her," Robert said as he and William lifted the captain into the coffin. "Not until you stand trial with her." He sealed the box.

One of the laboratories had been converted into a decontamination center. As trusted members of the ship's crew brought in the coffins containing the survivors from the mortuary compartments, Visitor doctors placed them into air-tight chambers, where most of the toxin clinging to their clothes was flushed out of the ship.

Mike and Julie watched as one of the doctors entered the chamber that now held Captain Jake. After a quick examination, he was given a sedative, then stripped. His clothes were stuffed into a box which would later be jettisoned.

The doctor left the compartment, it was flushed again, and the now-comatose captain was removed to another room where he could be given proper treatment while security could be assured.

"That one's a real prize," Julie said.

"In what way?" Mike asked.

"He was very visible on Earth," Julie explained, "at least in Los Angeles. And he's totally loyal to Diana, or at least to their Leader. If we can get him to talk under truth serum about the Visitor's original objectives, their plans, and the facts of conversion, and record all that, we could have a powerful tool to help convince people on Earth that our claims are true."

"That's a very good point," Mike said. "I'll go talk to Martin about that right now."

It was the middle of the morning at the suspension plant. National Guardsmen stood at their posts around the fence and at the doors to the building. High overhead was the descending form of a shuttle. When it landed, a lieutenant came out from the plant to stand in front of the shuttle's hatch.

Wary, armed, Mike Donovan and Martin descended from the shuttle.

"I'm Lieutenant Wallace, Mr. Donovan," the officer said. "I'm the commanding officer here, under direct orders from

Lieutenant Governor Dennis W. Simon. I and my men are to assist you in every way in the restoring of suspended human prisoners to life."

"I'm glad to meet you, Lieutenant," Mike said, extending a hand. "This is Martin, a Visitor and a friend."

"Pleased to meet you, Martin," Wallace said, shaking his hand too. "Have you brought technicians with you?"

"We have," Martin said as George, Annie, Joanna, and Phyllis descended from the shuttle, followed by two dozen other Visitors and four rebels. "Unless there was damage done to the machinery in the plant, we should have it operable within an hour or so."

"Excellent. You'll want to attend to those humans who were brought down previously first. I hope they're all still alive. I sincerely apologize for having interfered with their revival earlier."

"If any of them fails to pull through," Mike said, "it's not us but their families you'll have to apologize to."

"I'm aware of that, Mr. Donovan. Even though I was only following orders, I still feel responsible. I know it's no excuse, but my superior officers, and theirs too, haven't been exactly consistent in their instructions."

"That's the effect of conversion," Martin said. "Either directly or as a result of orders passed down from someone converted higher up."

"I understand that," Wallace said, "but I'm sure you understand that in both the government and the military, we get into the habit of doing what we're told, even if it doesn't make any sense. Hell, it almost never makes any sense. But those that don't follow orders soon find themselves weeded out."

"That's exactly why we're so concerned about convertees in positions of authority," Mike said. "And we've got plans on how to handle that too. But right here and now, these human suspendees are our primary concern. Are we going to have any problems with security?"

"I don't think so. A number of civilians are unhappy about that ship being up there in the first place, of course, and groups of vandals have tried to break in several times, with no success. Once we start releasing suspendees, our image will improve considerably."

"I sure hope so," Mike said.

"Can you give us a hand bringing more suspendees off the shuttle?" Martin asked. "The only other people we brought with us will be busy getting the machinery working."

"Certainly," Lieutenant Wallace said. He signaled to a sergeant. "Duty detail here, on the double," he ordered. The sergeant saluted and went to get his men in order.

They had the thirty coffins offloaded in short order. Then Mike and Martin went into the plant with the lieutenant while the four other rebels who'd come with them reboarded the shuttle to take it back up to the ship for another load.

Juliet Parrish and Barbara sat at the control board in front of the conversion chamber. Arnold, the master technician, and several other Visitors occupied the other chairs.

"We've never had to run the process backward," Arnold said, flipping switches. "No reason why it shouldn't work, however."

"We're going to need a guinea pig to work with," Juliet said. "And since I'm the only one here who's undergone conversion, I'm the logical choice."

"You can't take that risk," Barbara objected. "What if something goes wrong? The psychic shock of entering the chamber itself could be enough to damage you."

"I know that, and I don't like it. Just looking at that chamber brings back all the memories of what Diana did to me. But who else can we use?"

"I don't know," Arnold said, "but you're the one person who's keeping us all together. If anything happens to you, our whole organization will fall apart."

"Nonsense," Julie protested. "Mike can take over for me. Or Ham. Or Martin."

"Well, Mike maybe," Barbara said, "but he's not here now. And Ham may be competent at what he does, but people won't follow him the way they will you. And Martin just doesn't have the leadership potential. No, Julie, we're going to have to find another guinea pig."

"Please use a different term," one of the technicians said. "You're making me hungry."

* * *

The bulky blocks of machinery from which the conveyers emerged were only the tip of the iceberg. Putting humans into suspended animation required much more equipment than that, but most of it was concealed behind the walls against which the machines stood. But it was at the machines that the controls were located, and it was there that the processes of the concealed equipment could be adjusted, changed, adapted, or reversed.

And hence it was there rather than in the recesses of the plant that the Visitor technicians labored. They were now working on the last machine. All the others were now in operation, albeit slowly until refinements could be made.

Martin stood by one of the lines, watching as human beings, naked and damp from the solution in which they had been stored, slowly moved past to be helped off the conveyers. Still befogged by the suspension process, they were not aware of their nakedness, felt no shame as rebels and Visitors helped them on with clothes.

These clothes had been provided by one of the larger chain stores in Los Angeles, which was taking full advantage of the situation. On the one hand, they were planning to claim the full retail price as a tax deduction. On the other, they were publicizing their contribution to promote their line. As far as the revivees were concerned, such things obviously didn't matter.

As each person was dressed, he or she was led to another part of the plant where the person was given stimulants, plenty of liquids, and a little solid food by volunteers from Pomona and other nearby towns. The revivees were still dazed, though by this time they had recovered their sense of self enough to be confused to find themselves in such a place.

Here, after their brief meals, they were queried about their identities, their addresses, and the names of relatives. Since most of them had lived in San Pedro, they had no one to take them home. Other volunteers manned a jury-rigged switchboard in an effort to find someone to take the people away. There was no more room in the local hospitals.

From outside the plant came the muffled sounds of angry

shouts. Having seen the shuttles descending time after time and then returning to the Mother Ship, a number of people had come to see what was going on. Some of them, not believing either the taped message the rebels had prepared or the assurances of the soldiers inside the plant, were convinced that Visitors were being smuggled back down to Earth to take over again.

Mike Donovan and Lieutenant Wallace stood in one of the windowed offices at the front of the building, watching the restive crowd outside. A corporal came up to tell them that some families belonging to the revivees had been found, and should be arriving even now.

"I think a demonstration is in order," Mike said. "Our own communications with the rest of the community aren't good enough. Bring out those revivees whose families have responded and any of those who can get about on their own."

Lieutenant Wallace nodded his approval of the suggestion, and the corporal went off to do as he was bid. He returned a few moments later with about twenty people. They were pitiful, in poorly fitting clothes, still confused, and frightened by being in a strange place. The noise of the crowd outside was not reassuring either.

The corporal had also brought a squad of armed soldiers with him. Under Mike's direction, these went out the front door first and took up positions of guard. The crowd quieted for a moment and then started muttering again.

Then, with Mike on one side and Lieutenant Wallace on the other, the twenty or so revivees filed out of the building and into the parking lot. Once again the crowd quieted.

"Some of you are here in answer to our phone calls," Mike said to the crowd. "We have some of your friends and family here. If you recognize someone, please come forward, identify yourselves, and take these people home."

"It's a fake," someone in the crowd called.

"Just another trick," someone else answered.

"No," a woman yelled. She forced her way through the mob. "Mother?" she cried. One of the revivees, an elderly Spanish woman, looked up.

"Rosita," she said. Her voice, audible to all, was perfectly normal, perfectly human.

"Mother," the younger woman beyond the front gate cried again. She forced her way through and ran to the older woman, folding her in her arms.

And now others came forward, recognizing familiar faces among the revivees. The crowd stood silent, and then a man stepped forward.

"What about those others?" he asked, pointing at the revivees for whom no friends or family had come.

"We haven't been able to contact their relatives," Mike said, "and we're filling up in here. Can you find someplace for these people to stay until they can get home again?"

"Sure," the man said. "We've got an extra room."

The mood of the crowd completely changed. Those who had insisted it was all a trick were silenced, sometimes with fists.

"Please," Mike said, "we still have nearly ten thousand people left to release. We need all the help we can get."

"You'll get it," a young man with unfashionably long hair assured him. "We'll spread the word."

"Can we get more guards?" Mike asked Lieutenant Wallace as they returned to the main part of the plant.

"I'm afraid not," Wallace said. "In spite of Simon's instructions, these were all I could get."

"We were lucky this time," Mike said. "The next time we don't have a relative out there, some fanatic could actually start shooting."

"I know," Wallace said, "but there's nothing I can do. The police are totally occupied with stopping looting and other disturbances in the city. And most of the rest of the Guard is helping out with fires, ambulance calls, and the like.'"

"We've got a call from Barbara on the Mother Ship," a rebel said, looking up from the communications equipment at the side of the plant. "We've got *two* shuttles coming down next time."

"Hell," Mike said, "we can hardly keep up with what they're sending us now."

"She said there's been a fault in one of the circuits up there," the rebel said. "They're going to have to start sending the suspendees down as fast as they can, before the retrieval equipment fails."

"Damn," Mike said. He went over to where Martin was conferring with several technicians about how to speed up the revival process, and told him the news.

"We're going to need more volunteers from the city," Martin said. "We can deprocess people pretty quickly, but we don't have any place to put them afterward." He looked hopefully over Mike's shoulder at Lieutenant Wallace.

"I'll find somebody," Wallace said, and went back to the front of the building.

The noise of the crowds was still coming from outside the back of the plant. It arose from people who hadn't witnessed the release of the revivees just moments ago. Suddenly the noise became louder and organized itself into a chant.

"What the hell's going on now?" Mike asked as he went to the sliding double doors to take a look.

Outside, approximately fifty people wearing red togas with gold head- and armbands were moving about in a kind of rhythmic dance. As they warmed to their chant, the words eventually became intelligible. "Un—pure—un—pure—the Earth—is ours—the devil—begone," they said over and over again.

"Just what we needed," Mike snarled.

The few Guardsmen who were there were unable to move the demonstration back outside the fence. The two shuttles that had just been announced appeared in the sky and slowly settled toward the landing area. But the cultists, seeing the arrival, moved so that they were underneath the two craft and whenever one of the shuttles tried to find another place to land, ran there too, keeping them from settling down.

The Guardsmen, fully aware of the urgency of the situation, stopped being gentle and started swinging rifle butts. The cultists responded with clubs of their own and shouts of "police brutality," "alien puppets," "death to the evil ones," until one of the shuttles fired a shot into the ground near the thickest of the fighting.

The cultists, not prepared for real battle, fled with screams of hatred and threats of retribution. Their reception by the crowd outside the fence was not uniformly sympathetic.

The shuttles landed, and with as many guards as he could muster, Lieutenant Wallace supervised the unloading of another sixty suspended humans.

The children of the rebels had been given one of the ship's larger lounges for their own playground. Victoria Cohen was supposedly supervising them in their play. In actuality, all she did was make sure that nobody hit anybody too hard, handed out cookies and beverages on demand, and made sure that they confined themselves to the lounge and the adjacent compartments instead off escaping into the rest of the ship.

Josh Brooks, Sean Donovan's friend from happier days in San Pedro, was not playing with the rest of the children. After all, he was fourteen now, and most of the others were considerably younger. Victoria felt sorry for him, and after a while she went over to sit down next to him.

"Gets kind of dull after a while, doesn't it?" she said.

"I guess so," Josh answered. He was tense, as if suppressing some kind of anxiety.

"Can you tell me what's wrong?" Victoria asked. She was only twenty-two, and was not completely comfortable in her role as supervisor.

"It's my parents, Miss Cohen," Josh said. "Mr. Donovan thinks they were brought aboard this ship when the Visitors raided San Pedro. Do you know if they've been found yet?"

"I don't think so, Josh. Mike's down at the plant. He knows your parents and would tell us if they had been revived."

"I keep wondering," Josh said. "Maybe they were put on another ship, one of those that got away."

Victoria wanted to be reassuring, but she knew that Josh would sense any false hopes and condemn her for them.

"I guess that's possible," she said. "But we're sending the suspendees down as quickly as we can, and they're reviving them as quickly as they can. It won't be much longer." She hesitated. "I guess it's the not knowing that's the worst part," she said.

"Yeah," Josh said.

"You shouldn't think about it. There's nothing you can do about it, and everybody else is doing the best they can."

"I know. But that's not all. Sean's mother might be here too, and he doesn't seem to care."

"Sean Donovan?"

"Yes. He just sits in his room. He's not even here right now. He's not the way he used to be. I'm afraid my parents, even if they're here, might turn out the same way."

"But your parents weren't converted, were they?" Victoria asked.

"No, I don't think so."

"Well then, when we find them, they should be just fine." But Josh's words had given her an idea.

The suspendees were being unprocessed rapidly. The shuttles were still bringing them down about four times as fast as they could be handled, but the technicians had smoothed out the revival process, and about fifty volunteers from Pomona, Montclair, Glass Mountain, and other nearby towns were doing a heroic task of getting people back on their feet and into the custody of trustworthy people, if not to their actual families.

Mike Donovan, sprawled out in one of the larger chairs in a front office, was roused from a badly needed nap by one of the technicians.

"We've got a call from Ham," the man said.

Mike hurried over to the communicator room and took the microphone from the rebel on duty.

"Ham, what's the news?"

"The proof that 'No news is good news' is a lie," Ham Tyler's voice said from the speaker. "Mike, I just can't find any trace of Diana anywhere. Whoever it was that took her away from that sanitarium left no tracks at all. And that means they were real professionals."

"No clue as to who they were?" Mike asked.

"None at all. These guys are so good, they could be colleagues of mine, for all I know."

"So what now?"

"To tell you the truth, Mike, I just don't know. If I don't learn something within the next twelve hours, I'm going to pack it in and come back to the plant."

"It's not like you to give up, Ham."

"Everyone's got his limits, Mike. You know how to get in touch with me." The speaker went dead.

"She must have found the right tool," the communications operator said.

"That's exactly what I'm afraid of," Mike agreed. He wanted a couple more hours' sleep, but he knew it would be useless to try. Instead he went back into the office area of the plant, where a TV had been set up and where a number of rebels and off-duty technicians were sitting. It was ten minutes past the hour, and Julie's recorded message was just concluding. The networks, yielding to the inevitable, had rescheduled their programming to take this interruption into account.

But instead of the next episode of *Dallas*, there was a special message from Dennis W. Simon, the Lieutenant Governor. This was one of the things people were watching for, so all small talk stilled.

"I am very happy to tell you," Simon said into the bank of microphones, "that at last report, nearly two thousand human prisoners have been brought down to Earth from the Mother Ship, and that of those, nearly five hundred have been revived and returned to their familes."

"An exaggeration and out of date at the same time," Martin said, coming in to stand behind Mike.

"I wish to extend my heartfelt thanks," Simon was saying, "to all the people, both human and Visitor, who have been working so hard to liberate these victims.

"However, I must deplore the actions of a few, who have been trying to impede the speedy release of our citizens." Behind him were several other people, slightly out of focus. "I ask you, I beg you, to cooperate with the brave men and women, and with the National Guard, who are doing their best to bring our loved ones home to us."

"He's awfully damn slick," someone said.

"Even more sadly," Simon said, "a number of our citizens have taken this time of crisis as an opportunity to loot, to rob, and to create crippling public disturbances. I implore you all to—"

"Wait," Martin said, moving up closer to the screen. He turned down the volume, then pointed to one of the men directly behind the Lieutenant Governor, a heavyset man with a particularly thick head of hair. "That's one of the men who came to the sanitarium to speak to Diana," he went on.

"Well, goddamn," Mike said. "Are you sure?"

"Watch the way his eyebrows work. Yes, I'm sure."

"What do you know?" Mike said. "Ham will love this. Those guys weren't so sharp after all. Diana's in the governor's mansion."

Chapter 12

Juliet Parrish stared at Victoria Cohen-in shocked dismay. "You can't be serious," she said. They were sitting in the conversion lab, Barbara and the others watching as they talked.

"But I am," Victoria insisted. "Sean was converted, and quite successfully too. He doesn't even *know* he's been converted, so that makes him a perfect subject."

"But he's only a child," Julie protested. "We can't experiment on a child."

"He's fourteen, old enough to be a man. Besides, if we don't figure out how to deconvert people, how many other children will suffer?"

"I don't like it, Victoria."

"You don't have to like it. You've told us yourself, sometimes you have to sacrifice the few for the sake of the many."

Juliet looked at the younger woman. Sean had been involved that time too, held on this ship, and she'd roundly criticized Mike for running the risk of trying to rescue him. "All right," she said. "Will you bring Sean in here?"

"He's right outside," Victoria said, going to the door. She opened it and Sean came through. He smiled brightly enough, but his movements lacked a certain energy.

"Hello, Sean," Julie greeted him as he came over to take a chair next to her. "How have you been?"

"Oh, just fine," he answered. His words were bright, his expression happy, but it was all false. There was nothing underneath.

"What do you know about conversion, Sean?"

"Nothing." No curiosity, just a flat statement.

"This is the room where it's done," Julie said, turning to look at the glass-enclosed chamber where she had once undergone such torture. "I'm sure you remember it."

"No, ma'am."

"Maybe he never saw it from here," Victoria said. "Come with me, Sean," she said, and led him through the side access up to the conversion platform itself.

"Oh," Sean said when he was inside. "Yes, now I remember—sort of."

"What do you remember, Sean?" Julie asked.

"Diana was sitting there where you are, and there were other people, and she made all these pictures come into my head. It was sort of like a dream, but I was awake at the same time. It was very real. I liked it, but I've forgotten most of it."

"That was part of the conversion process," Victoria said gently.

"Was I converted?"

"Yes," Julie said, "we think you were."

"Let's go back out there and talk about it," Victoria said, and led Sean down to the control console again.

"Seems like an awfully expensive way just to make dreams," Sean said as he took his chair.

"It does more than that," Julie said. "It changes your mind for you."

"It didn't change mine," Sean said.

"Do you like baseball?" Victoria asked.

"Nah," Sean answered, taking the non sequitur in stride. "I think it's dumb."

"Do you remember how you felt about it last week?"

"I guess I thought it was dumb then too."

"Can you remember your last birthday?" Julie asked. "What did your father get you?"

"A baseman's glove."

"Think about it, Sean. Think about how you *felt* when you got that glove."

Sean looked at her, and for the first time since he'd come back from the ship, there was some depth to his expression, more than just surface questioning and doubt.

"I—I used to like baseball a lot, didn't I?" he said at last.

"A real hard-core fan," Julie said.

Sean's gaze turned inward for a moment. Julie could see his composure begin to crumble, then she watched as he pulled himself back together by sheer force of will. "No," he said. "They didn't do anything to me."

"Yes they did, Sean," Julie said, "just like they did to me. We think we can undo the conversion, make you and me both like we were before. You want to try?"

"Yes," he said simply, surprisingly without any hesitation. "When can we do it?"

"Right now," one of the technicians said. "Come with me, and we'll get you prepped." He led Sean through a side door.

"Oh, boy," Julie said, sitting back with a sigh of released tension. "If we hurt Sean and Mike finds out, we're all going to be in bad trouble."

"I know," Victoria said, "but if Sean is deconverted, then we'll have a chance of saving our world after all."

The last few shuttles had carried more than just suspended people down to the processing plant. Helping to unload the coffins were a few rebels who somehow didn't get back up to the ship again. Ham Tyler and Mike Donovan had consulted after the discovery of Diana's hideout, and had decided that though they could probably trust Lieutenant Wallace, it would not do to advertise a gathering of strength.

At last they were ready with a core of twenty hardened fighters, all human but armed with the best Visitor weapons. They met in a parking garage where Ham had stored the fast vans that would take them to Sacramento. They had decided that a shuttle seen moving in that direction would give up any surprise advantage they might have.

Robert Maxwell was the last to arrive, bringing with him not another rebel but an older man whose manner bespoke propriety and authority, though his clothes were not what he might have been accustomed to.

"Who's that?" Elias Taylor asked. He and Sancho Gomez and Thomas Lee would be going up in the first truck.

"This is Sidney Carvelle," Robert said. "He's one of those we revived up on the ship."

"And I'm more than grateful to you," Carvelle said. His voice was measured and cultured. "Under the circumstances, I see that it is only my duty to assist you in your enterprise."

"What can you do for us, Mr. Carvelle?" Grace Delaney asked while Fred Linker looked on.

"I was chief of domestic staff at the governor's mansion," Carvelle answered. "You might need some assistance in finding your way around inside."

"Maxwell," Ham said, "you're a genius."

"Pure luck," Robert said, "but better than that, with Carvelle's help we were able to locate the Governor himself, Abe Riggsbee."

"I don't like what I've seen of Simon lately," Carvelle said with carefully concealed disdain. "Mr. Riggsbee should relieve him of his responsibilities."

"Unfortunately," Robert said, "Riggsbee's not a well man. They're doing what they can for him up at the ship now. Caleb will bring him down in a small shuttle as soon as he's able to travel. But we can't coordinate with him until he arrives."

"Then we're going to have to just do what we can," Mike Donovan said. "We'd better get moving. We've got a long drive ahead of us."

Diana sat with Dennis Simon in a superbly furnished parlor in the governor's mansion.

"Professor Mauritz at Berkeley," Simon told her, "has just informed me that he's been able to reproduce the antitoxin."

"That's excellent," Diana said. "Then the blood samples we sent him did the trick?"

"Exactly. There was too little antitoxin in your own blood to do them any good, but Richard, being a survivor, had a fully developed spectrum of antibodies—whatever that means."

"That means that Joyce won't have to wear her respirator

any longer, once we get a supply of the antitoxin here. And I won't have to wear the damned thing at all. How long till supplies arrive?"

"They sent a car from Berkeley even as Mauritz was phoning," Simon said, "so it shouldn't be too many hours."

"Diana," a feminine voice called from a side door. It was Zenia. "Colonel Fletcher is here."

"I'll be right there," Diana called to her companion, then turned back to Simon.

"Do let me know as soon as the antitoxin comes in," she said, getting to her feet. Then she went through the door from which she had been summoned.

Beyond was a short corridor off which opened several doors. Zenia stood in one of these and stepped aside so that Diana could enter.

Seated around the table were Colonel Fletcher and three other officers. Diana nodded and took her place at the table, Zenia sitting at her right. A moment later two other Visitors entered to join them, a woman in a respirator and a man whose human disguise looked as if it didn't fit him too well.

"All right, Colonel," Diana said, "we are ready to begin. You know Joyce and Richard." This was said for the benefit of the Major, whom Diana had not met.

"I do," the colonel said. "And this is Major Garret. You've met Captain Broadbent and Lieutenant Casey."

"Now that the formalities are disposed of," Diana said with a small smile, "can you get the weapons?"

"A bit abrupt, aren't we?" Major Garret said tightly.

"Why take a thousand flowery words to say what can be said in ten plain ones," Diana retorted. She turned back to the colonel.

"We can," Colonel Fletcher said in answer to her previous question. "Captain Broadbent has secured two mobile rocket launchers, three tanks, several heavy machine guns, and other mobile artillery—nothing too heavy but plenty big enough for what we want to do."

"That's excellent, Captain," Diana said. "Then I'm sure we'll have no difficulty capturing a shuttle."

"We know their schedule," Lieutenant Casey said. "We estimate they will have brought down the last of the suspendees sometime tomorrow. Our observers will note any subsequent variation in activity at the plant."

"It will be interesting to see what real American firepower can do against Visitor technology," Major Garret said.

"You'll have plenty of opportunity to find out," Diana said, "*after* we get hold of one shuttle intact."

"I intend to take all three intact," Garret said, "or as many as are on the ground when we attack. But if I know these rebels, they won't accept a simple coup. And if they fight back, I'll just blow them away."

"Should have been done long ago," Richard said. His face looked as if the person under the mask had lost weight.

"I agree," Diana said. "I have a personal bone to pick with several of the rebels, but I think I'll have to forgo any satisfaction. When taken, they are to be killed immediately."

"Abrupt again?" Garret asked. Only this time his wry sense of humor was more evident.

"As abrupt as I have to be. I'm sure, Major Garret, that your weapons can do all you say they can. But there are heavier guns on board the Mother Ship as well. Except to shoot down one balloon, these have never been fired on your planet. We won't have won until we regain control of the ship and of those weapons as well."

"That will put you into an incredibly strong position," Colonel Fletcher said. "I'd like some reassurance that you'll keep your end of our bargain."

"I can't carry out the next step without your help," she said. "The Lieutenant Governor should do anything you tell him, even if you don't have direct control over him as I do. Given him as your starting point, you'll soon have control of the whole state. Playing from the background is not my way, but if you can stomach it, then you should very well succeed."

"I'd much rather have true power and anonymity," Colonel Fletcher said, "than the appearance of power and publicity."

"I agree," Garret said, "and I'm sure Broadbent and Casey do too. It's easier to control the masses if they don't know who's doing the controlling."

"If we make a mistake," Broadbent said, "we just switch figureheads and try again."

"Then you should have no trouble gaining control of the

state legislature," Diana said. "You'll need some of my people to help you with that until we can learn how humans can telepathically communicate with each other."

"The important thing," Joyce said, speaking for the first time through her respirator, "is that we turn all this bad feeling about Visitors into at least tolerance."

"It's ironic," Richard said, "that the broadcasts from the rebels are emphasizing the same thing. They're playing right into our hands."

"We've been noticing an improvement in your public image already," Lieutenant Casey said, "except, that is, for you personally, Diana. You're too strongly identified with what happened before. Nobody will believe that you'd turn around and become Earth's friend."

"That will be no problem," Diana said. "We can change these faces we wear if we wish. Richard will need a new one, in any event. Once we regain control of the ship, I'll assume a new face, a new identity, that will be known only among the eight of us here."

·"Won't people suspect something when a new person shows up?" Lieutenant Casy asked.

"A number of Visitors have died," Diana said. "I'll just pick the identity of one of those."

"And you don't like to work from the background," Captain Broadbent murmured.

"I don't like it, but I'll do it if I have to."

"I think we ought to mix strategies too," Colonel Fletcher said. "Until we have complete control of the legislature, have weeded out those who could cause us trouble, and replace them with our own people, I think we ought to have our Lieutenant Governor extend martial law. That way I can act up front in my regular capacity."

"I will put the weapons on board my ship at your disposal," Diana said, "though they should probably not be used too often, or we'll destroy our credibility."

"I agree," the colonel said, "and if used, there should be plenty of supportive publicity before and after. But it's not California I'm worried about. It's the President, and the Congress and the Senate."

"We've already made some tentative inquiries in that

direction," Lieutenant Casey said. "It may take two months to make all the contacts, but several Visitors are already in position and only need coordination and direction."

"And once you have the President of this country under your control," Diana said, "then you shouldn't have too much difficulty with other governments around the world."

"Not if we act carefully and secretly," Colonel Fletcher agreed. "I foresee complete control within three years."

"And then," Diana said, "you must cooperate in letting us take more water back to our own world."

"I thought the toxin the rebels spread had spoiled everything for you," Captain Broadbent questioned.

"The animal life, yes," Joyce answered, "but water can be purified and filtered."

"But if I understand your situation correctly," Garret objected, "you need so much water that you'll turn Earth into a desert, and then what good will that do us?"

"Compromises must be made," Diana said. "We can restrict ourselves to just the water that is in your ice caps. If we're careful, you won't even notice any changes in your coastlines."

"And besides," Richard continued, "once we're back on our feet again, Our Leader will be far more amenable to considering an alliance between us. By combining our technologies, we should be able not only to defeat Our Leader's enemies, but also insure your continued mastery of this planet. And there are other planets, you know."

"And that, Colonel Fletcher," Diana told him, "is what makes your cooperation so valuable. I think Our Leader can get along very well with a man like you."

Chapter 13

A wheeled medical cot had been placed in the center of the conversion chamber. Sean, naked and relaxed, lay on the cot. They had done it this way instead of making him stand up during the process because Juliet Parrish, Barbara, Arnold, and the other conversion technicians had wanted to reduce tensions in the boy, not increase them.

Strange lights from overhead played on the small figure. But they were soothing lights, not the wild, frightening flashes Juliet remembered. At the controls the technicians were feeding thoughts directly into Sean's mind, amplifying his memories of his father's love and care, easing his conflicts over betraying the rebels' false plans to Steven.

"It's slippery," Arnold said, fine-tuning a dial. "The effects of conversion are so recent, so spurious, that I can't get hold of them securely enough to counter them directly."

"If anything even *starts* to go wrong," Julie said nervously, "we stop at once."

The technicians bent to their delicate task. On the cot in the chamber, Sean whimpered softly.

Three hours north of Los Angeles, on the long road to Sacramento, the rebel caravan of vans pulled over to the side to change drivers. The pause lasted only five minutes, then they were on their way again.

In one of the vans, Grace Delaney listened to the communicator, using earphones so that the other rebels with her could rest. Mike Donovan stretched out on the seat beside her, ready to catch a moment's sleep, when she prodded him gently.

"It's Martin," she said. "Governor Riggsbee has just been brought down."

"How is he doing?" Mike asked softly.

Grace whispered into her microphone. "Weak," she said after listening for a moment, "but game. He'll be coming up as soon as he can."

"I hope he makes it," Mike said.

"I'm more concerned about Chris," Alice Reynolds said from the back of the van. "I know he and Gorf are friends, but I just don't trust that motorcycle gang."

"What choice do we have?" Mike asked. "Besides, they came through for us before."

The lights in the conversion chamber went out one by one. And one by one the exhausted technicians sat back in their chairs. On the cot, Sean stretched once and sat up.

"How do you feel?" Juliet Parrish asked him through the communicator.

"Just fine," Sean said. "Those were pretty good dreams."

"I'm glad you enjoyed them," Arnold said as a technician entered the chamber, carrying a robe to cover Sean's nakedness.

"I did, but I'm glad they're over. Is Josh around?"

"He's with the other children," Victoria said. "Shall I call him?"

"Yes, please, and tell him to bring his mitt. I'd like to play some catch."

He stared at them in surprised confusion as everybody cheered.

Spotlights at the corners of the governor's mansion lit the surrounding grounds in the predawn darkness. At Sidney

Carvelle's suggestion, the rebels had secured a house from which they could observe the mansion easily. Police patrolled the grounds, but there had been little public disturbance up here, and they had little cause for alarm.

From a third-story window, Carvelle was pointing out key locations to Mike Donovan and Robert Maxwell, while Ham Tyler coordinated what they saw with the rough sketch map Carvelle had prepared earlier. There was no way their small force could just occupy the place. The mansion was too large and complex, and there were too many police as well as contingents of National Guardsmen close by. They were going to have to make a quick raid, search only those rooms in which Carvelle thought Diana might be staying, and then get out again.

They were interrupted when one of the rebels let in a large man wearing black leather pants and a leather vest and with greasy hair down to his shoulders.

"Are you Smiley?" Ham asked, looking up from his map.

"Yeah, and you're the Fixer. Chris says hello." He reached out a hand darkened with motorcycle oil, and Ham shook it.

"What do you have in the way of weapons," Mike asked, coming over from the window.

"Not much—a few pistols, small stuff."

"Can you get him something?" Mike asked Ham.

"Not at this late date," Ham said. "How come Chris didn't find you guns?"

"We decided not to be too obvious," Smiley said. "We've got our plan all worked out, and only need to know time and place."

"You've got a radio?"

"Chris has it."

"Then we'll let you know, but it will be within the next hour or so. Carvelle?"

The older man came over to the table and was introduced.

"Show Smiley where you want his boys to be," Ham told him.

"Okay," Carvelle said, took the sketch map, and went with the biker to the window to point out the place he'd chosen.

"Is that it, then?" Ham asked Mike.

"I think so. Robert, anything more you want to add?"

"Nothing. Let's start getting into position. There's just enough traffic out there that we're going to have to move one at a time."

"All right," Ham said. "If everybody knows what they're supposed to do, let's get moving."

The sky was just turning pink. The police officers stationed in front of the mansion had another hour yet before change of duty. It had been a dull night as usual, and they were bored.

Then a grubby biker driving a chopped hog that had only glass packs for mufflers drove up the far side of the street, stopped, and turned his bike so he was facing the mansion. He didn't turn off the machine. He just sat there, occasionally revving the engine.

One of the policemen walked to the edge of the grounds and shouted across the street at the biker. "What do you want?" he said. "Move along."

But the biker just sat there. Another biker, this one dressed in denims with fringes, came up from the other end of the street but also on the far side, and parked his bike next to the first. He too just sat there, staring at the mansion, occasionally revving his engine.

Two other officers joined the first. After exchanging glances, they drew their sidearms. "You'd better get moving," the first officer said.

"Shooting unarmed people now?" the second biker asked. His hands were on the handlebars. He was wearing no gun.

The officers, not quite sure what to do, just stood there as two more bikers in black leather came up, one from either side, and turned their bikes parallel to the first two. They too repeatedly revved their engines, and after a moment all four were revving in unison.

One of the officers went toward the mansion to summon a superior while several others, hearing the noise, came from either side of the building. Two more bikers joined the group across the street and sat there, watching, smiling, just twisting the throttles on their handlebars.

"You're going to have to move along," the first officer shouted above the noise.

"It's a public street," one of the bikers called back. "And we're public," another one added.

The sergeant, summoned by the officer, came out of the mansion just as four more bikers, two from either direction, came to take their places beside the first group.

"What's going on out here?" the sergeant called.

"We just came to look," the original biker said. "Curious about the place where all those stupid bulletins are coming from."

"You're causing a public disturbance," the sergeant shouted. "Now, either you move along or I'm going to have to call in reinforcements."

In response, four more bikers roared up, taking up positions near the ends of the block. The sergeant backed off a pace, looking from one sardonic grin to another. Behind him, policemen from the far side of the building were gathering, guns drawn, ready for they knew not what.

"Somebody call the National Guard," the sergeant said.

As if that were the cue they'd been waiting for, all the bikers burst into motion, roaring across the street and onto the grounds, swerving to dodge the police's fire and running an occasional officer down. For a few moments there was total chaos. The police were afraid to fire lest they hit one of their own officers. The bikers, gunning their engines hard and swerving wildly, tore up the lawn roaring through the frantic and dodging police.

And just as suddenly, the whole gang turned almost in unison and sped off, weaving to avoid being shot. The police, rattled by the sudden and bizarre attack, were less than effective. No cyclists fell.

When the rebels heard the rhythmic revving of motorcycle engines change to a constant roar, they leapt from their hiding places behind the mansion and ran toward the now unguarded rear entrance. The door was locked, but Carvelle had his key out, and within half a minute, they were all inside with the door shut behind them.

Quickly they moved past the kitchens and staff offices toward the main part of the building. There were no police inside. They had all gone out to join in the melee, the noise of which was clearly audible. Following the plan they had rehearsed, they rushed up the main stairs to the second floor and started going into the rooms, one of which, they hoped, would contain Diana.

The few sleepy staff, awakened by the noise, were quickly silenced and locked away, though some of them recognized Mike Donovan and grinned encouragement at him. But though the rebels found Lieutenant Governor Simon and his wife sitting up terrified in bed, there was no sign of Diana.

"Try the third floor," Carvelle said as they heard the bikers riding furiously away.

Ham Tyler, Grace Delaney, and Thomas Lee ran up the back stairs while the others kept silent, hoping to put off discovery for yet a few moments longer. After what seemed like an eternity, Lee came back to the head of the stairs.

"She *was* here, I think," he said, "but it looks like they left sometime last night."

"They couldn't have known we were coming," Robert Maxwell said. "The police would have been ready for us if they had."

The front door opened downstairs. Mike and Sancho Gomez looked over the railing to the foyer below and saw a slightly battered police officer going toward one of the side offices.

"Just a matter of seconds," Mike whispered. "We're not going to get out without a fight."

"I think the cavalry just came," Elias Taylor said. He was standing by a window at the front of the building, from which he could see the police slowly regaining order on the torn-up lawn below. Sidney Carvelle came to join him.

Out in the street, a big Lincoln limousine was drawn up to the curb right in front of the entrance. Half a dozen state highway patrol cycles stood propped nearby. The other rebels came forward to see the chauffeur get out and open the back door. The mansion police had stopped their activity and were watching too as first a nurse, then a man in a three-piece suit got out. They turned to the car door and helped another man from the back seat.

"It's Riggsbee," Carvelle said. "The cavalry indeed, and ours to boot."

Riggsbee straightened, leaning on the nurse and the man for support. As he stepped away from the car, the figure of Caleb Taylor emerged, dressed like a normal civilian for a change, but still carrying his sidearm.

Riggsbee spoke to the mansion police. The rebels couldn't hear what he was saying, but the sergeant saluted sharply while the highway patrol closed in around the Governor, the nurse, Caleb, and the other man, and escorted them to the door.

They heard the front doors open below them. "All right, Mr. Donovan," they heard Riggsbee call. His voice was determined but weak because of his illness. "No need to shoot. I'm on your side."

Chapter 14

It was a strange party in the main parlor of the governor's mansion. The Governor, his doctor and nurse, and three highway patrolmen sat or stood at one end of the room. At the other end were Mike Donovan, Ham Tyler, Robert Maxwell, and several other rebels. To one side was the Lieutenant Governor, half dressed, and the sergeant and two officers of the mansion guard.

"I want you to know," Governor Riggsbee said, "that I am very grateful for all you have done, Mr. Donovan." He looked at a very confused Dennis Simon. "I have been assured by people on the Visitors' ship," he went on, "that unlike my friend here, my mind has not been tampered with."

"Can you give us any proof of that?" Ham asked suspiciously.

"No, I cannot, but when I spoke with Martin at the plant where all the human captives are being revived, he told me to give you a message which might lend some credence to my words in general. You have a son, Mr. Donovan?"

"Yes," Mike said hesitantly.

"His name is Sean, I believe. Miss Parrish, working with a Visitor named Arnold—" He hesitated until Mike nodded recognition of the name. "Miss Parrish sends word that Sean likes baseball again."

"Oh, my God!" Mike said, his voice breaking. He turned away, covering his face with his hands.

"I don't know what that means," Riggsbee said, "but I see that you do."

"It means they've figured out how to reverse the conversion process," Robert Maxwell explained.

"Ah, then there's hope for us yet," Riggsbee said. "I'm very glad to hear that, considering all I've heard during these last few very long hours. Well, Mr. Donovan, do you trust me?"

"Yes," Mike answered, turning back and struggling to regain his composure.

"Very good," Riggsbee said. "Then with your permission, I will resume my position here. Martin has been good enough to entrust me with one of your communicators, which is following in another car. As soon as it arrives—and I get a little rest—I will establish contact with your people at the plant and begin to contact people I can trust in the state government. Mr. Simon has thoughtfully left us in a state of martial law, so I should have no difficulty—once I know who I can trust—reestablishing order again. Only this time, it will be human order, not Visitor order."

"An awful lot of those Visitors are our friends now," Robert said.

"I know that, and I appreciate their sacrifice. But until we know that our world is truly safe, no Visitor is going to be left where they will have any chance of influencing people in authority. Except of course, the suspension plant and your ship."

"This is all well and good," Ham said, "but restoring you to office, Mr. Riggsbee, was not our primary intention."

"I'm aware of that. It's just a most fortuitous side benefit. So, then, have you found our true enemy, this Diana?"

"No," Mike said, "she was here but now she's gone."

Mike Donovan turned to the police sergeant who was standing behind Simon's chair. "We're pretty sure Diana was here," he said. "Did you see her?"

"No, sir. I was on duty from ten o'clock last night. I'm pretty sure I'd recognize her if I saw her."

"Mr. Simon," Mike said, "she was here, wasn't she?"

"Ah, yes, yes, she was. She was here yesterday. I know because I spoke with her, uh, about, uh—"

"All right," Ham Tyler said. "So where is she now?"

"I don't know. She and her friends had rooms on the third floor. Aren't they there?"

"If *this*," Governor Riggsbee said, "is how covertees act when their leashes are cut; then we are in serious trouble indeed." Simon stared at him. "Dammit, Dennis," Riggsbee said. "You were a competent man once."

"It's not his fault," Mike said.

"I know, but I depended on Mr. Simon for a lot, and without his help, I'm not sure I'll be able to handle the job alone."

"We can find somebody for you," Ham said. "But right now, the real question is, where's Diana?"

"Maybe she and her friends left before Sergeant Binkley came on duty," Riggsbee suggested, looking up at the parlor door where Chris Faber was quietly slipping in.

"No way," Chris said. "My biker friends were watching this place since about noon yesterday."

"Well, then," Ham said, "who *did* leave here, and when?"

"That Colonel Fletcher," Chris said. "He and his staff marched out around midnight."

"Yes," Simon said. "I'd forgotten about him." He seemed to be trying to think, to clear his memory. "Fletcher, Broadbent, Casey, and Garret."

"That's four," Chris said. "There were five in his group, according to Smiley. The colonel, a major, a captain, a lieutenant, and a sergeant."

"There was no sergeant here," Simon said, "except for police sergeants, of course."

"How much you want to bet Diana was that sergeant?" Robert asked.

"No takers," Mike said. "It had to be her." He turned to the Lieutenant Governor. "But you said she had some friends with her?"

"Yes, three Visitors, a man and two women. The man's face looked funny, wrinkled like."

The police sergeant suddenly looked guilty.

"We let three of the cleaning staff out at four this morning," he said. "One of them was a man with a strangely wrinkled face."

"Goddamn it," Tyler swore, "they *can't* have known we were coming."

"I don't think they did," Mike said. "I think they had some other plan of their own."

"But why would she want to leave?" Robert Maxwell asked. "She was in control here. Everything was going her way."

"Not quite everything," Sergeant Binkley said. "Most of the staff didn't like her much."

"If I were her," Governor Riggsbee said, "I'd want to be in my own office. That's why I came all the way up here from Los Angeles."

"The ship?" Mike asked. "But she does't have a shuttle."

"There were three shuttles at the suspension plant when we left," Riggsbee's doctor said. "They'd been parked there for quite some time."

"And over eight thousand helpless human hostages inside the plant," the nurse said, her eyes wide.

"And a tame colonel," Ham added, "who has access to National Guard armaments."

"And there's practically nobody left at the plant to defend it," Robert said.

"All right," Ham shouted, "you get the picture. Let's get a *move* on!"

They were half an hour out of Sacramento before Grace Delaney remembered that she could call the ship from her communicator. Her message was terse and to the point—they needed a shuttle, now, and told them to home in on her signal.

Another half hour later the appearance of the shuttle threw traffic on the freeway into a panic. Peter was at the controls. The rebels abandoned their vans and climbed on board. Another half hour later and the silent and surrounded plant was below them.

"That damn colonel's good," Ham Tyler said from his seat beside Mike Donovan. Ringing the plant were a dozen pieces of heavy military hardware, including tanks and rocket launchers. Armed troops stood between the armored vehicles, manning machine guns, mortars, bozookas, and similar infantry equipment.

Inside the surrounding fence, the paved plant yard was empty except for the three shuttles.

"Diana wants at least one of those shuttles intact," Mike said, "but if I know Martin, he's got people inside them, manning the weapons."

Mike set his own, smaller shuttle down inside the plant yard but well away from the other three Visitor vehicles. As Mike stepped out of the hatch, a door at the side of the plant opened and Lieutenant Wallace stepped out. The two met under the watchful eyes of the surrounding enemy.

"It's a stalemate," Lieutenant Wallace said. "If we shoot at them with the shuttle guns, they'll start blowing up the plant and all the suspendees inside." He nodded at a heavy tank which was aimed just over their heads. "I know that equipment," he went on. "This building would be rubble in minutes."

"Sounds like we'd better talk with their commanding officer," Mike said.

"Colonel Fletcher is around in front," Wallace told him. "He wouldn't believe you weren't here until we told him where you'd gone. That seemed to amuse him for some reason."

"I'll bet it did," Mike muttered. He started toward the building, and Lieutenant Wallace fell into step beside him.

Inside, Martin met Mike by one of the processing lines. The equipment had been stopped, and there were forty or fifty revivees standing around.

"We've got a clear line to the Mother Ship," Martin told him. "What do we do now?"

"That's just what I'm going to find out," Mike said. He left Martin, went through the hallways to the front lobby, and stepped out the front door. Parked just inside the front gate was an army command car with two men inside, one behind the wheel and one in the back.

Mike Donovan came well clear of the door and waited while the passenger of the car got out. It was Colonel Fletcher.

"I understand," Fletcher said, "that you've been visiting up north."

"That's right," Mike answered. "You probably passed us on our way up there."

"Very likely. Five vans in a row?"

Mike nodded. "Next time I'll phone ahead," he said. "You're really taking this business seriously," he went on, waving at the armored vehicles and troops that stood outside the fence.

"Very seriously indeed, Mr. Donovan."

"So what did you have in mind, Colonel. We've got over eight thousand civilians in there, you know."

"I'm very aware of that. Indeed, that's why we're here. I have someone with me who thinks you might have stolen her ship. Her terms are quite simple. You give her her ship back, or we blow up the plant and everybody in it."

The meeting took place on that very spot, halfway between the front door of the plant and the gate where Colonel Fletcher's car still stood. On one side stood Mike Donovan, Martin, Ham Tyler, Robert Maxwell, and Grace Delaney. Behind them a dozen or more other rebels kept watch at the windows, ready for any signs of treachery.

Just two paces from them, with the might of the National Guard behind them, stood Colonel Fletcher, Major Garret, Captain Broadbent, Lieutenant Casey—and Diana.

"You've given us quite a chase, Diana," Mike said. "From halfway to the moon all the way back to here."

"So it would seem," Diana said, "but the chase is over now. It's really quite simple. I want my ship back."

"Do you think that we're just going to hand it over to you?" Ham demanded.

"You will do exactly that," Diana said, "if you don't want all those people in there to die."

"How can you go along with this?" Mike asked the colonel angrily. "Can't you see what she's doing? You should be holding her in custody so she can be made to answer for her crimes."

"Crime is a matter of definition," Colonel Fletcher said, "a definition usually provided by those who win the war."

"And what about us?" Martin asked Diana. "There are a lot of us on the ship who have no desire to follow you any further."

"Those of the crew," Diana said quite matter-of-factly, "who wish to remain on this poisonous planet may come down with the rebels. I don't really care what happens to you, but I intend to return to our home world, and to Our Leader."

"I'm sure he'll welcome you with open arms," Martin said sarcastically, "unless, of course, those who get home first tell him *why* this world was spoiled for him."

"I'll deal with that when I get home," Diana said, not the least flustered by his remark. "The worst that could happen there would be preferable to staying here. Now, make up your minds. Do you vacate the ship and let me return aboard, or do I start shooting up the plant?"

The colonel, without turning, gave a hand signal to someone behind him, and the tank that stood a dozen yards beyond his car swiveled its turret, taking aim at the side of the building just beyond where the rebels inside were watching the proceedings.

"What's to be gained by this?" Ham Tyler demanded.

"More than you might think," the colonel said calmly.

"Make up your mind," Diana insisted.

"I don't think you'll do it," Mike said, still looking at the colonel.

Fletcher smiled softly, raised his hand again, and the tank pumped a high explosive round into the side of the plant. The shell penetrated the outer wall, then exploded, sending shards of concrete high into the air. Mike and his friends flinched while the rebels inside scrambled for cover. Colonel Fletcher, however, stood unmoved.

"If I'm going to die here," Diana said while the rebels gazed in shock at the destruction behind them, "I might as well take everybody here with me. It won't be as satisfactory as blowing up your whole world, of course."

"I can't believe you," Mike said in dismay.

"I can," Ham said. "If she'd do this, think of what she would do if she got her ship back."

Diana grinned, the colonel signaled again, and a second round exploded next to the first. This time part of the second story caved in.

"All right," Mike said, "that's enough."

"You can't be serious," Ham exclaimed.

"We haven't got a chance," Mike said through gritted teeth. "Even if we could get the shuttles up, she'd kill us all before we could do her people any significant damage. And then her friends here will have no serious competition. So all right, on the chance that we might be able to fight later, I'm willing to give in now."

"That's very smart of you," Diana said. "I don't intend to give you a second chance, of course."

"There's one condition, though," Mike said.

"And what's that?" Colonel Fletcher asked.

"That while we're bringing down the rest of our people and any Visitors who want to stay here, we also disassemble the doomsday device, so Diana can't reactivate it and threaten us with it again."

"Why, certainly Mr. Donovan," Diana said, smiling broadly.

Diana and Colonel Fletcher watched as Mike Donovan and the other rebels rejoined their companions in the damaged plant, then turned and walked toward a command trailer the colonel had set up just outside the fence. Colonel Fletcher dismissed his staff as he let Diana precede him into the trailer.

"What's this about a doomsday device?" he asked calmly, flopping into a chair. The trailer, though in military colors, was comfortably furnished, with a kitchen at one end and a communications center occupying most of the rest.

"A ploy that failed," Diana answered. "The only thing it accomplished was that it gave me time to escape when they invaded the ship just before the departure of the rest of the fleet. Which, in itself, turned out to be rather useful, since if

I'd been in their custody then, I would not have had the opportunity to make your acquaintance." She smiled at him as if she found him more than a little attractive.

"Will you have wine?" Colonel Fletcher asked, getting to his feet and going to a cabinet in the kitchen end of the trailer.

"Yes," Diana said after an infinitesimal hesitation. "I would like that. A celebration, yes, to our victory. Once I'm back on board my ship with only loyal crewmen, that victory will be assured."

"Those rebels will still be on the loose," Colonel Fletcher said, pouring red wine into two white-wine glasses.

"The very first thing I will do," Diana said, accepting the glass, "will be to destroy this plant utterly, and all who remain within it, which should take care of Mr. Donovan and the rest of his rebels—and the traitors—quite nicely."

"What about my troops?" Colonel Fletcher asked, returning to his chair.

"Surely, Colonel, you will have pulled them all back out of danger by then. As a token gesture to our rebel friends of our good intentions, of course."

"And the suspendees in the plant?"

"How many people, Colonel Fletcher, are you willing to kill to gain mastery, not just of this country but of the whole world?"

"As many as is necessary," Colonel Fletcher said, smiling.

"The important thing," Diana said, "is that none of those rebels survive. They nearly defeated me once, and I suspect, if you gave them a chance, that they would cause you more than a little trouble. Also, except for those of my people who specifically agree to cooperate with you, all the fifth columnists must die. They can help your present government against us by divulging too much about our science and technology. You are going to have a difficult enough time of it as it is without any further competition."

"You said you intended to return to your Leader," Colonel Fletcher said, subtly changing the subject.

"Indeed I will, but only after you are in control. There's no sense my going back and returning with ships for water, only to find that I'm being met by enemies on Earth. Rest assured,

Colonel, I'll support you to the limit of my abilities. My own profit is at stake as well."

"I don't suppose you'd object to me and my staff accompanying you to your ship," Fletcher said.

"Colonel," Diana said, raising her glass, "I think that would be a pleasure for both of us."

Chapter 15

The great Mother Ship's command center was all but deserted. Only Barbara and an electronics technician remained, carefully removing the doomsday device from the control panel. Those crew members whose sympathies lay with Earth had long since been sent down to the suspension plant near Pomona, while those who chose to remain loyal to Diana were still locked in their quarters. Only a few fifth columnists and rebels remained on the ship to make sure it was secure and that nobody had been left behind.

Victoria Cohen, one of these few, came in, her face frantic. "Robin and Elizabeth haven't been accounted for," she said.

"Are you sure?" Barbara asked, carefully snipping wires.

"I've just called down to the plant, and they're not there," Victoria said. "Sean and all the other children were the first to go."

"Well, don't tell me about it," Barbara snapped. "I'm sorry, it's just that this won't be really safe until all the connections are cut. You'll have to go looking for her, that's all."

Victoria closed her eyes and sighed. "All right," she said. "I'll see you at the docking bay."

She hurried out of the command center and, not knowing where else to look, went back to the cabin where Robin Maxwell had been staying. The girl hadn't been there the last time Victoria looked, and she wasn't there now. Almost crying

181

with anxiety, Victoria hurried to the docking bay where Barbara and the technician were just handing the detached device up to Paul Overbloom, standing in the hatchway of the last shuttle.

"I can't find them," Victoria cried. "I don't know where to look!"

"Everybody else is on board," Paul said. "Diana won't tolerate any more delay."

"We'll use the ship's communication system," Barbara said. "Wherever she is, she'll hear us."

"Why didn't I think of that before?" Victoria wailed, but even as they left the shuttle, Robin came running in from one of the ship's corridors.

"I can't find Elizabeth," Robin cried. "I told her we were leaving, and she said something like *'shemma terion,'* and ran off. I've looked everywhere."

"*'Shemma terion?'*" Barbara repeated. "That means 'toy blocks.'"

"Of course," Robin said. "When Elizabeth was up here before, Diana gave her a set of bright transparent blocks to build cities with."

"But Diana's room has been sealed off for days," Victoria protested.

"You don't know Elizabeth," Barbara said. "Locks mean nothing to her. We'd better hurry."

Barbara stopped along the way to get a key, and when they got to Diana's quarters they found the door still locked, as Barbara suspected it might be. The key worked, however, and inside they found Elizabeth at Diana's lounge table carefully and calmly packing the brightly colored transparent blocks into a box which had obviously been intended for some other purpose.

"Oh, Elizabeth!" Robin cried, running to grab up her daughter. "I was so worried about you."

"Well, it's all right now," Barbara said, jumbling the rest of the blocks into the box any which way and closing the lid. "Now come on, we've got to hurry."

* * *

Twenty minutes later, the shuttle bearing Elizabeth Maxwell and the last of the rebels and fifth columnists descended to the paved yard behind the suspension plant.

There were two reception parties waiting for them. Colonel Fletcher, his staff, and a hand picked squad of soldiers stood surrounding Diana while, facing them just paces away, were Mike Donovan, Robert Maxwell, Juliet Parrish, Ham Tyler, Chris Faber, and Martin.

As if knowing what was expected of them, the shuttle landed so that its hatch, when it opened, would be between the two groups.

"That's the last of them then," Diana said.

"The rest is all yours," Mike said grimly.

The hatch of the shuttle opened and Paul Overbloom stepped out, followed by Barbara, then Robin leading Elizabeth and finally the others. When she saw her father, Robin rushed over to hug him. Elizabeth sedately carried her box of blocks as she followed her mother right past Colonel Fletcher.

Diana gave the colonel a sharp glance, and he reached down and picked Elizabeth up in his arms. The little girl did not protest or cry out.

"What are you doing?" Julie asked sharply.

"Just a hostage," Colonel Fletcher said.

"No!" Robin screamed, and if it hadn't been for her shocked father's restraining hands, she would have flung herself on the colonel. Before Mike or Martin could make a move, the soldiers surrounding Diana raised their weapons.

"What is the meaning of this?" Mike demanded. "That's not part of the deal."

"It is now," Diana said while Robin wailed and struggled in her father's arms. "We need this child, to learn the secret of your antitoxin."

She and the colonel and his staff, with the soldiers keeping guard, began to move toward the shuttle. Elizabeth, calm and dispassionate as ever, swung her box, the lid came open, and the crystalline blocks scattered through the air.

On board the ship, in the subdued light the Visitors preferred, they had been beautiful enough. But here in the full light of day, with Earth's brilliant sun blazing down, they sparkled and shimmered in a blinding rainbow of color. The soldiers, taken by surprise and dazzled by the prismatic effect of the tumbling blocks, broke formation in order to cover their eyes. And Elizabeth, with calm deliberation, turned and with a flick of her reptilian tongue, spat venom full in Colonel Fletcher's face.

The colonel's scream of pain caused his soldiers to turn their attention to him instead of to the rebels, who lost no time in taking advantage of the momentary distraction. Robin, breaking free of her father at last, ran to her daughter while Mike, Robert, Ham, and Martin dashed in to grapple with the colonel's staff. The soldiers, afraid to hit one of their officers, dared not shoot.

Diana started to run toward the shuttle, but Juliet was faster. She ran four steps, then jumped, just barely catching Diana's legs with her outflung hands. It wasn't much of a tackle, but Diana stumbled, her glasses fell from her eyes, and she cried out in pain as the bright southern California sunlight blinded her.

It gave Julie the chance she needed to regain her feet, grab Diana, and twist her arm behind her back so forcefully that the confused soldiers could hear the Visitor's shoulder joint creak. The scene froze like a tableau.

Rebels and staff officers were too closely entangled for the soldiers to do anything more than raise their weapons in idle threat. Mike Donovan, holding the colonel, managed to draw his pistol and put it to Fletcher's head.

"Just hold your fire," he said to the soldiers, "or your colonel's dead."

"Destroy the plant," Diana screamed, struggling in Julie's determined grasp. "Now!" Julie twisted her around and struck her hard across the face. Diana slumped to her knees, her human disguise half torn off, revealing the green scales underneath.

"Look!" Julie said, turning her captive around so that the soldiers could see her true face. "This is who's been giving your colonel orders."

Beyond the fence the tank commanders, who had been instructing their crews to aim at the plant, hesitated.

"There are eight thousand human beings in there," Robert Maxwell called, holding Lieutenant Casey in a stronghold.

"That's a lie," Major Garret shouted. "Just a few rebels, that's all."

Once again, the barrels of the tanks, the batteries of the mobile rocket launchers began to swivel for direct fire.

Then the double doors of the plant opened, and out came a hesitant trickle, then a stream of revived suspendees. Dazed, confused, in ill-fitting clothes, they formed an ever-growing huddle on the paved yard.

Beyond the fence, an officer picked up a bullhorn.

"Lower your guns," he called.

Captain Broadbent, held securely by Martin, stared at the pitiful human ex-prisoners. Then, craning his neck so he could see Colonel Fletcher, he said, "You didn't tell us about this."

"Forty people," Colonel Fletcher said, still half blinded by the venom, "fifty people. What does that matter when the whole country, the whole world is at stake?"

More suspendees came out of the plant, slowly filling the area between the building and the fence.

"They've been continuing with the deprocessing the whole time," Mike Donovan said in wonder.

"Seemed like a good idea," Martin said, slowly releasing his hold on Broadbent.

The tank officer who had stopped the attack on the plant started directing his soldiers to come to the suspendees' aid. As word spread among the soldiers, they lowered their weapons and began to back off. The stream of suspendees was slackening now, but by Mike's estimate, fully three hundred humans were now standing out in the plant yard. Their numbers slowly diminished as those who had been instructed to help them started leading them away.

A squad of MPs dogtrotted out to where rebels and staff officers still stood in frozen postures of struggle and resistance. The soldiers nearby fell back, seeing master sergeant's stripes on the MP's leader. The Military Police knew their business and soon had Colonel Fletcher and his staff disarmed and in handcuffs.

"That sure is some secret weapon," the master sergeant snarled at Broadbent as he took him into custody.

"Colonel Fletcher told us," Captain Broadbent explained, "that you had a nuclear device in that building." He looked at Lieutenant Casey and Major Garret, whose grim faces told him they had not been deceived. "At least," Captain Broadbent went on, "that's what he told me."

A major, leading another squad of white-helmeted MPs, marched across the yard from the gate in the fence. Beyond them, soldiers who were not actively engaged in assisting the suspendees were drawing back. Colonel Fletcher and his men were marched off, leaving only the rebels, and Diana still firmly in Julie's grasp, to meet the new officer.

"I think we can take this lady off your hands now," the major said, indicating Diana. "If I had known that she was behind Colonel Fletcher's orders, it never would have gone this far."

Four MPs, all the size of football tackles, went over to Diana and handcuffed her securely. She looked bizarre, with one-half of her face still that of a beautiful woman, the other half that of a green, scaly reptile. The MPs, not liking to touch such a being, were not gentle.

"There will be no convenient escapes this time," Juliet said as a security van rolled up to them. "We'll see you again, at your trial."

Diana was roughly loaded into the van. The major saluted and marched his men off the field.

Mike and Julie and the others turned to leave as well and saw Robin and Elizabeth sitting on the pavement. Elizabeth had constructed a fanciful tower out of her crystal blocks. It gleamed like fire in the sun.

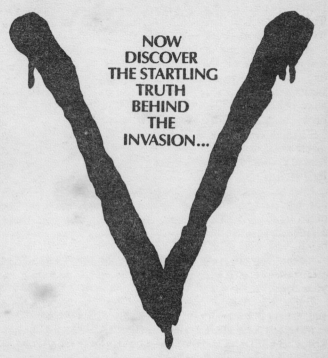

YOU WATCHED IT ON TV...

NOW
DISCOVER
THE STARTLING
TRUTH
BEHIND
THE
INVASION...

...as the ultimate battle for survival continues...

BESTSELLERS FROM NEL

'V'   A. C. Crispin   £2.50
V: EAST COAST CRISIS
   Howard Weinstein & A. C. Crispin   £2.50

AND WATCH FOR

The Chicago Conversion

the next V book from New English Library

All these books are available at your local bookshop or newsagent, or can be ordered direct from the publisher. Just tick the titles you want and fill in the form below.

Prices and availability subject to change without notice.

NEL BOOKS, P.O. Box 11, Falmouth, Cornwall.

Please send cheque or postal order, and allow the following for postage and packing:

U.K.—55p for one book, plus 22p for the second book, and 14p for each additional book ordered up to a £1.75 maximum.

B.F.P.O. and EIRE—55p for the first book, plus 22p for the second book, and 14p per copy for the next 7 books, 8p per book thereafter.

OTHER OVERSEAS CUSTOMERS—£1.00 for the first book, plus 25p per copy for each additional book.

Name ....

Address ....

....